She'd let things get *out of* control.

Tell him the truth. Tell him Brody's his son. Do it now, a stern voice inside her head commanded.

But she refused to hear that voice. Instead, she put out a hand and warned him softly, "Don't say any more. Please."

He captured her wrist, the movement so swift, she had no chance to jerk away. For a frozen moment, they looked at each other, a look so deep, she felt as if she was falling....

And then, with slow care, he brought that fist to his mouth and brushed his warm, soft lips across the top of her clenched knuckles.

Before she could collect her scattered wits and pull away, he let her go. "Sorry," he said. "I guess I'm moving a little too fast, here."

She started to protest, to say, *It isn't that,* but stopped herself. He'd only ask, *What is it, then?* And there they'd be, back with the one thing she couldn't tell him....

Dear Reader,

We're deep into spring, and the season and romance always seem synonymous to me. So why not let your reading reflect that? Start with Sherryl Woods's next book in THE ROSE COTTAGE SISTERS miniseries, *The Laws of Attraction*. This time it's Ashley's turn to find love at the cottage—which the hotshot attorney promptly does, with a man who appears totally different from the cutthroat lawyers she usually associates with. But you know what they say about appearances....

Karen Rose Smith's *Cabin Fever* is the next book in our MONTANA MAVERICKS: GOLD RUSH GROOMS continuity, in which a handsome playboy and his beautiful secretary are hired to investigate the mine ownership issue. But they're snowbound in a cabin...and work can only kill so much time! And in *Lori's Little Secret* by Christine Rimmer, the next of her BRAVO FAMILY TIES stories, a young woman who was always the shy twin has a big secret (two, actually): seven years ago she pretended to be her more outgoing sister—which resulted in a night of passion and a baby, now child. And said child's father is back in town... Judy Duarte offers another of her BAYSIDE BACHELORS, in *Worth Fighting For*, in which a single adoptive mother—with the help of her handsome neighbor, who's dealing with a loss of his own—grapples with the possibility of losing her child. In Elizabeth Harbison's hilarious new novel, a young woman who wonders how to get her man finds help in a book entitled, well, *How To Get Your Man*. But she's a bit confused about which man she really wants to get! And in *His Baby to Love* by Karen Sandler, a long-recovered alcoholic needs to deal with her unexpected pregnancy, so she gratefully accepts her friend's offer of her chalet for the weekend. But she gets an unexpected roommate—the one man who'd pointed her toward recovery...and now has some recovering of his own to do.

So enjoy, and we'll see you next month, when things once again start to heat up, in Silhouette Special Edition!

Sincerely yours,

Gail Chasan
Senior Editor

Please address questions and book requests to:
Silhouette Reader Service
U.S.: 3010 Walden Ave., P.O. Box 1325, Buffalo, NY 14269
Canadian: P.O. Box 609, Fort Erie, Ont. L2A 5X3

CHRISTINE RIMMER

LORI'S LITTLE SECRET

Silhouette®

SPECIAL EDITION®

Published by Silhouette Books

America's Publisher of Contemporary Romance

For my guys…again and always

SILHOUETTE BOOKS

ISBN 0-373-24683-8

LORI'S LITTLE SECRET

Copyright © 2005 by Christine Rimmer

This edition published by arrangement with Harlequin Books S.A.

® and TM are trademarks of Harlequin Books S.A., used under license.
Trademarks indicated with ® are registered in the United States Patent
and Trademark Office, the Canadian Trade Marks Office and in other
countries.

Visit Silhouette Books at www.eHarlequin.com

Printed in U.S.A.

Books by Christine Rimmer

CHRISTINE RIMMER

came to her profession the long way around. Before settling down to write about the magic of romance, she'd been everything from an actress to a phone sales representative to a playwright. Christine is grateful not only for the joy she finds in writing, but for what waits when the day's work is through: a man she loves, who loves her right back, and the privilege of watching their children grow and change day to day. She lives with her family in Oklahoma. Visit Christine at her new home on the Web at www.christinerimmer.com.

THE BRAVOS:
HEROES, HEROINES AND THEIR STORIES

Chapter One

What are the odds? Lori Lee Billingsworth Taylor couldn't help wondering, feeling guilty and miserable and knowing herself to be a yellow-bellied coward.

What are the odds she would keep running into a certain man? Given that the town—Tate's Junction, Texas—where this certain man constantly turned up had a population of almost two thousand. Given that Lori was not—oh, no, definitely not—trying to run into this particular guy. At least not yet.

The odds couldn't be all that great, could they?

But still, it kept happening. Lori Lee kept running into Tucker Bravo.

And she did know. Oh, yes, she knew very well, thank you very much, that Tucker Bravo was exactly the man she *needed* to run into. Unfortunately, he was also the man she couldn't bear to face.

But she would. She truly would.

Right after her twin sister's wedding.

It happened first at the Gas 'n Go.

Lori and her ten-year-old son, Brody, had just arrived in Tate's Junction from San Antonio for a three-week stay. Not five minutes in the town she'd left behind—and there *he* was.

What, she asked herself later, had made her stop for gas? She might just as well have kept going straight to her parents' big two-story brick house on Pecan Street. She had over a quarter of a tank and could have filled up later. But she turned off the highway and there was that bright red cube of a convenience store and the eight gas pumps and it just seemed so simple, so easy and efficient, to go ahead and gas up right then.

Brody, busy on his Game Boy in the back seat, spoke up as she stopped the Lexus at the pump. "I bet they have Icees in there."

She turned and gave him a fond smile. "That would be no."

"But, Mom—"

She grabbed her purse, bent to tug the latch that opened the gas tank door. "We'll be at Gramma Enid's in ten minutes tops."

"Gramma Enid doesn't have Icees."

"Sit tight." She unhooked her seat belt and reached for the door.

"Aw, Mom…" But another glance over the seat

showed her he was already focused on the Game Boy again, thumbs flying over the miniature keyboard.

Lori paused, her fingers hooked in the door handle, staring back over the seat at her son's bent head, thinking that they were doing okay, just the two of them, without Henry...

Henry...

A wave of sadness washed through her. Henry had died a little over a year before. Lori missed him and so did Brody. But time was doing its work. Lori had made it through the worst: the clutching desperation, the gaping, ragged hole of emptiness at the center of her world. Increasingly, thoughts of Henry brought only a fond sort of sorrow. They'd shared six wonderful years, she and Henry—seven, if you counted the year before their marriage. Lori would always have her warm and comforting memories of those years. She was a fortunate woman; she had a smart, healthy son and she'd known the quiet joy of a good man's sure and steady love.

Lori tugged on the door handle and swung her feet to the pavement. She shut the car door behind her and was fiddling in her purse for her wallet when she heard the urgent whining sound.

She glanced up. The ugliest, most adorable dog she'd ever seen sat near the rear wheel, big brown eyes begging her, long wiry-haired body quivering.

The dog captured her gaze and held it, whimpering louder, lifting up to all four stumpy legs and wiggling all over in barely contained excitement, as if it had been waiting all its life to run into someone like her.

Lori couldn't help herself. She laughed. "Where did *you* come from?"

It was all the encouragement the funny-looking dog needed. Panting in sheer doggy bliss, it quivered on over to her and rolled to its back.

"Okay, okay." Lori crouched to scratch the spotted, wiry-haired pink belly. Transported, the dog whimpered and wriggled, pink tongue lolling. "Yes, you are about the cutest thing I've ever seen," she declared as she went on scratching. "But no, I can't take you home."

"You wouldn't believe it to look at him now, but he already has a home." The voice, from behind her, was male: deep and sure, threaded with amusement.

She turned her head—and there *he* was, standing in the sun beyond the shadow of the roof that protected the pumps, big arms folded over his deep, hard chest, strong legs braced slightly apart, spiked brown hair catching golden lights from the bright Texas sun overhead.

Tucker.

Oh, God.

He was…bigger, somehow, than she remembered. That formerly whipcord-lean body spoke of muscular power now. The hungry, wild-eyed yearning look was gone from his dark eyes.

Lori felt her stomach heave. She swallowed, hard, and pasted on a wide smile. Ordering her suddenly numb legs to straighten, she stood to face him.

That killer smile of his widened. "Lori Lee," he said, without having to hesitate to place her—and also without confusing her with her twin, Lena Lou. "I knew it was you the minute you got out of that gorgeous car."

Lori supposed it wasn't surprising, that he remembered her on sight. He'd once been in love with Lena Lou. Lena was the sparkly one, the popular one. All the boys went nuts for her. Lori had been quieter, a better student, and a little bit shy. Though they were identicals, no one in town had ever had any trouble telling them apart.

Except for on that one special, magical, life-changing night—which she was not going to think about, at least not right now.

Tucker said, "It's been a long time."

Lori nodded and gulped to clear her clutching throat. "How are you, Tucker?" It came out sounding pleasant. Cordial in a distant sort of way. Most important, her tone betrayed no hint of the turmoil within.

Before he could answer, the dog at her feet let out a long, impatient whine—a clear demand for more attention.

Tucker commanded, "Fargo, you shameless mutt, get over here." One last whimper for good measure, and the dog waddled over to its master. It plunked itself down next to Tucker's booted feet as he answered her question of a moment before. "I'm good. Real good."

She kept her pleasant smile in place, though it took superhuman effort to do it. She felt giddy, disoriented—and terrified. Nothing seemed real, suddenly, as if when she'd turned to see him standing there, she'd spun into the midst of a strange dream, a dream that hovered on the verge of nightmare. She thought her smile would crack, her lunch rise up and come spewing out her grinning mouth.

Talk, she thought. Say something. Now. "I, um, heard you did just what you'd always dreamed of do-

ing. Traveled all over the country. And even Europe—
Spain and Italy and England…"

"You heard right." He bent to give the dog a scratch
behind a floppy ear and she thought of all those times,
in the early years, that she'd tried to reach him.

Every time she'd drummed up the courage to make
contact, she found he'd moved on. In Austin, a stranger
answered his door. The tortured letters she'd written
him explaining everything came back with no forward-
ing address.

Tucker straightened to his height again. "And look at
me now. Right here in Tate's Junction where I swore I'd
never end up." He grinned wider. "Believe it or not, I
did manage to get myself a law degree during my wandering years."

"Ah," she said, as if that meant anything.

He went on. "Got me the whole South Wing out at
my mean old granddaddy's house and an office on Center Street with a sign out front that says, Hogan and
Bravo, Attorneys at Law. And, last but no way least, I've
got Fargo here." He grinned down at his goofy-looking
dog, then back up at her. "And you know what?"

She did know. She could tell just by looking at him.
"You're happy."

"You bet I am."

Behind Lori, the left rear door of the Lexus clicked
open. Oh, no, she thought. *God. Please. No.* Her heart
leapt into her throat and got stuck there.

"Mom?" Brody spotted the mutt. "Aw, sweet. A dog."
He was all the way across the seat and out of the car before she could find her voice to tell him to stay put. The

dog, spotting another sucker, gave Brody one of those pleading, hopeful whines.

Lori cleared her throat. "Brody…"

But he was already sliding past her, making a bee-line for Tucker's ugly dog. "Hey boy, hey buddy…" The dog whined in joy and Brody dropped to his haunches, right there at Tucker's feet. The dog licked his face and Brody hugged him and patted him and scratched him behind both ears.

Lori looked up and found Tucker watching her. A shiver went slicing through her, so cold it burned. "My son," she said, and she could hardly believe that her voice didn't so much as waver. "Brody Taylor."

"Hey, Brody," said Tucker.

"Hey," Brody replied, hardly glancing up, his whole being focused on petting the dog. "What's his name?"

"Fargo," Tucker said.

Lori looked from her son to Tucker and back to her son again. Oh, sweet Lord, she could see it. See Tucker in Brody—in the way he tilted his head. In the shape of his jaw.

In that distinctive cleft in his chin…

She shut her eyes and dragged in a hard breath. When she opened them again, Tucker was looking right at her.

He frowned. "You okay, Lori?"

"Oh, uh, fine. I'm just fine."

"Sure?"

"Oh, yeah. So. You like it here, in Tate's Junction, after all."

"Yes, I do—you're in town for the wedding?"

And to tell you about Brody. Before I leave, I will *tell you.* "That's right. For the wedding."

Lena Lou had finally found the man she wanted to marry. His name was Dirk Davison. Like Heck Billingsworth, Lori and Lena's father, Dirk sold cars. He owned two big dealerships on the outskirts of nearby Abilene. Dirk had proposed to Lena a year before.

"Going to be quite an event, that wedding," Tucker said.

"Oh, yes." Ever since she'd got Dirk's four-carat ring on her finger, Lena had been planning the biggest, most elegant, high-dollar wedding that Tate's Junction had ever seen. Lori reached into her purse again and came up with her wallet. "And we'd better get moving." She flipped the wallet open and slid out a platinum card.

"Well," said Tucker. "Great to see you again…"

"Yeah," she answered, keeping her fake smile firmly in place. "Brody…"

Brody scratched the dog some more. "Aw, Mom…"

"Come on. Back in the car." Lori stuck the credit card in the pump slot as Tucker clucked his tongue at the dog.

"See you later, Brody," Tucker said, turning. The dog fell into step behind him.

"Bye, Fargo." Brody rose and stared after the man and the dog as they headed around the convenience store, most likely on their way to the pumps on the other side. Once they disappeared, Brody looked at his mother. "Cool dog."

Relief flooded through her. She'd made it through meeting up with Tucker again. He'd even seen Brody. And nothing terrible had happened. Her knees felt like strings of overcooked spaghetti. She braced a hand on the gleaming hood of the car.

"Mom. You okay?"

She drew herself up. "You bet."

"We should get a dog, Mom. I could take care of him. You wouldn't have to do anything 'cept pay for his food."

"Nice try," she said wryly, though she was thinking that maybe he was right. Maybe he *was* ready for a puppy and all the responsibility that came with it. But she'd been a mother long enough to know that if she told him now, she'd never hear the end of it. "Want to help me pump this gas?"

"Sure."

As Brody unscrewed the gas cap for her, Lori told herself she didn't need to even think about Tucker again—not until after the wedding.

Not until she made herself call him and set up a time to tell him what she should have told him years ago.

It happened again the next day. Sunday.

In church, of all places, which just made Lori feel guiltier and more cowardly than ever. Her eleven-year deception seemed all the more reprehensible when she had to confront it while sitting in the Billingsworth family pew with those two big pictures of a dewy-eyed Jesus behind the altar looking down on her reproachfully.

In church. It was the last place she'd expected she might see him. The Tucker Bravo she remembered from all those years before never went to church.

Organ music filled the high-ceilinged sanctuary as folks settled into the rows of pews. To Lori's right, beyond Brody, Lori's mother, Enid, and her dad, Heck, nodded and murmured hellos to the friends and neighbors who filed past on the way to their own seats.

Lena sat to Lori's left, with Dirk on her other side. Lena's auburn hair fell in soft waves to her shoulders and her face seemed to glow with happiness. She and Dirk were holding hands, constantly turning to look at each other, sharing secret smiles and goo-goo-eyed glances of mutual adoration.

Lori probably wouldn't have believed it if she hadn't seen it for herself. But now she *had* seen it. She knew it was true: for the first time in her mostly self-absorbed twenty-eight years, Lena Lou Billingsworth was in love. Not since high school, when Lena was so gone on Tucker, had she ever lavished so many bright smiles and enchanting glances on a man. And with Tucker, there had always been as many scowls and pouts as there had been smiles.

With Dirk, Lena was all shining eyes and happy grins. Dirk Davison, no doubt about it, was the man Lena had been waiting for all her life.

Lena's fiancé was thirty-five, big and beefy and gruffly good-natured—a whole lot like Heck Billingsworth, as a matter of fact. Both men had broad, always-ready salesman smiles. They both laughed too hard and talked too loud and sometimes made you wonder if they actually heard a thing you said.

"He's just like Daddy," Lori had whispered to her twin the day before, after being introduced to the jovial Dirk.

"He is," said Lena, looking pleased as a little red heifer in a field of tall alfalfa. "Exactly like Daddy."

Lori just didn't get it. How could her twin fall so hard for a man so much like their dad?

But then, Lena didn't have the issues with their father that Lori had. Lena, after all, hadn't gone and gotten herself pregnant at the age of seventeen by a mystery lover whom she staunchly refused to name.

Heck had blustered and ranted and delivered all kinds of scary threats and ultimatums when he learned that Lori was pregnant. But Lori never did tell him who her baby's father was. She couldn't bear to tell anyone—for a number of reasons.

And when he finally realized she would never tell him, Heck had packed her off to stay with his sister, Lori's dear now-deceased Aunt Emma, in San Antonio—as if they were all living in the dark ages or something. As if it was the ultimate shame on a family, for a daughter to have a baby without getting herself a husband first.

Eventually, Lori had found happiness in San Antonio. She'd gone to work for Henry and married him and Henry had always treated Brody as his son. Though Lori didn't make it home to Tate's Junction much, she and her father had pretty much made peace with each other.

But that didn't mean she'd ever *marry* someone like Heck. Uh-uh. No way. Never in a hundred million years.

But Lena was doing just that and apparently couldn't have been happier about it.

Lori found Lena's love for her car salesman fiancé truly weird—as well as yet another example of the many ways she and her identical twin were nothing alike. She slid a glance at the two love birds to her left just as Dirk raised the hand he had twined with Lena's and pressed his fleshy lips to it. The two gazed deep into each other's eyes.

Just as Lori was reminding herself not to stare, Tucker appeared in the aisle, directly in her line of sight. Her stomach did a nasty roll. She blinked. Tucker spotted her—and he winked.

Why? she wondered, feeling sick and suddenly desperate. Why would he wink at her?

Oh, please, she argued with herself, as she actively resisted the powerful urge to leap to her feet and stumble along the pew away from him, not caring whose feet she stepped on as she made her escape. *Why shouldn't he wink? What does it matter? He's just being friendly, for heaven's sake.*

"Mom." Brody's skinny elbow poked into her ribs. "Look," Brody whispered. "It's the guy with the cool dog. Tucker."

She almost—*almost*—turned and snapped at her son to be quiet. But she caught herself just in time. "Yes," she said, with marvelous calm, considering the tangled, frantic state of her emotions at that moment. "It's Tucker." She raised her hand and gave Tucker a wave.

He waved back—and then he moved on by.

"Sure did like that dog of his," said Brody wistfully. "Hope I see that dog again…"

Lori stared after Tucker, though she knew she shouldn't, admiring in spite of herself the wide set of his shoulders, the proud way he carried his tawny brown head. He slid into a pew near the front, with his older brother, Tate, and Tate's pretty blond wife of ten months,

Molly. Molly's family was also there: her mother, her mother's husband, her grandmother and a tall, thin old fellow that Lori didn't recognize.

After church, the Billingsworths went to Jim-Denny's Diner for sandwiches. Tucker showed up there, too—with Tate and Molly. The Bravos and the Billingsworths ended up in adjoining booths.

Molly leaned over the seat and gave Lori a grin. "Hey. Good to see you, Lori Lee."

"Hi, Molly."

Molly had been three years ahead of Lori and Lena in school—and one year ahead of Tucker. Molly grinned at Brody. "This your boy?"

"Yes. Molly, this is Brody."

Tate Bravo's wife reached right over the seat, grabbed Brody's hand and shook it. Molly owned a hair salon. She was the mayor of Tate's Junction and the mother of twin babies, a boy and a girl. She was also the most unlikely person ever to have married someone like Tate Bravo.

On his mother's side, Tate—and Tucker, too, of course—came from the most important family in the area, the Tates. For generations, the first born Tate son had been given the name Tucker. Since Tate and Tucker's mother, Penelope Tate Bravo, was the only child of the last in a long line of Tucker Tates, she'd named her first son Tate and her second, Tucker, keeping the family name alive in her children. Everything had gone to her sons when she passed on. The Bravo boys now owned at least a part of just about every business in town, not to mention a sprawling ranch called the Double T on which stood a ranch house the size of a king's palace.

Molly had been born in a double-wide trailer. She came from two generations of single-mother O'Dare's. She was, truly, the last person anyone ever expected Tate Bravo to marry.

But Tate *had* married Molly, last summer. Their romance had been rocky, to say the least. According to the stories Lori's mother and sister had told her, Tate and Molly had the whole town buzzing there for a while. But now they were blissfully happy together.

Lori was happy *for* them.

She only wished they hadn't taken the booth next to the one her family sat in—at least not if they had to bring Tucker along.

And why did she have to end up sitting directly opposite him? She actually had to make a conscious effort to keep from looking straight at him.

Molly asked about the wedding. And Lena—with Enid chiming in now and then—launched into a long list of things that had yet to be done, from more floral consultations to final fittings of bridesmaids' gowns to a few changes in the menu for the sit-down dinner for three hundred at the local country club. Molly would be doing the bride's hair. Lena wouldn't have it any other way.

As the women talked wedding preparations, the men discussed Cadillacs. Evidently, Tate, who owned a fleet of them, was buying a new one from Heck. Dirk was contributing his expert advice.

Tucker sat silent, as did Lori and Brody, the three of them outsiders in the two current topics of conversation—looking right at each other, but too far apart to start up a conversation of their own.

Which was just fine with Lori. What would she *say* to him? Talking to him, making meaningless chitchat, seemed so evil and wrong when there was Brody right beside her, the son he didn't even know he had.

Tucker kept sending her glances—and she kept glancing back.

Well, how could she help it? Unless she stared at the table, he sat square in her line of sight.

Every time he caught her eye, she would picture herself standing straight up in that booth and announcing, *Okay. All right. The truth is, it was me, on prom night eleven years ago. Me and not Lena. You made love to* me. *And it's not some stranger, like everyone thinks, who's Brody's dad. It's* you, *Tucker. Brody's your son.*

Of course, she did no such thing. But the urge to do it was there, and it was powerful. It burned beneath her skin. It was that scary, exhilarating feeling you get standing on the edge of a cliff, wondering, what would it be like?

To stretch out your arms and slowly fall forward, to let yourself soar right off the edge…

The waitress—not Molly's mother, Dixie, who had worked at the diner since long before Lori left town, but was apparently off that day—brought the food. Though her stomach seemed tied in a series of permanent knots, Lori had never been so grateful to see a cheeseburger in her life. It gave her something to do, something to look at—other than Tucker's velvety-brown eyes and handsome face.

Brody took a couple of bites of his grilled cheese sandwich and then set the sandwich down. "So where's Fargo?" he asked Tucker, loudly, turning in his seat, causing the parallel conversations of Cadillacs and weddings to stop.

Heck laughed. "Fargo." He frowned. "The boy mean that ugly mutt of yours, Tucker?"

Tucker nodded. "'Fraid so—and Brody, Fargo's not welcome at church, or here at the diner. I haven't got a clue why not. He loves a good sermon as much as the next dog."

"His table manners aren't so hot," suggested Tate.

"I sure liked that dog," said Brody, sending Lori a calculating glance.

"Kid wants a dog," Heck said to Lori, as if she hadn't already figured that out for herself.

She looked at her father. "Got it." It came out too sharp. Between the state of her nerves after ten minutes of sitting straight across from Tucker, and the way her father always made her feel as if she wasn't quite the mother she ought to be…

Well, she was getting a little bit edgy.

Her dad spoke gently—and with clear reproach. "Now, Lori-girl, a boy should have a dog."

"Yeah," said Brody eagerly, and launched into the arguments all kids have ready when it comes to getting a pet. "I'm ten now. I'm old enough. Like I said, I could take care of everything, Mom. I'd feed him and walk him and clean up all his messes. You wouldn't have to do *anything*."

Lori set down her fork without eating the bite of potato salad at the end of it. She sent her father a narrow-eyed, not-another-word kind of glance and she told her son, "Brody. We'll discuss it. Later."

"But, Mom, I—"

"Later."

Brody got the message. At last. He picked up his sandwich and dutifully bit into it.

There was a moment or two of awkward silence. Then the men went back to their talk of fancy cars and Lena returned to the subject closest to her heart—her upcoming wedding.

"I just cannot believe that it's almost here. All our planning and hard work, and in two weeks from yesterday, I'll be walking down the aisle at last...."

Heck stopped talking Cadillacs long enough to remark, "'Bout damn time, too. My checkbook can't take too much more of this."

Lena laughed her bright, bubbly laugh. "Oh, Daddy. Just you wait. I'm gonna make you so proud."

"You already do, baby. You always have."

Lori looked down at her barely touched food and knew there was no way she could eat another bite. The conversation ebbed and flowed around her—and she didn't want to look up.

But she couldn't stare at her plate forever.

She lifted her gaze.

And found Tucker waiting, looking right at her.

The corner of his beautifully shaped mouth quirked up, a half smile that was also, somehow a question.

She felt the answering smile lift the edges of her own mouth.

This couldn't be happening.
And yet, somehow, impossibly, it was.
Tucker Bravo was flirting with her.

Chapter Two

That night, Tucker made a clear and calculated effort to get his sister-in-law, Molly, alone.

He had dinner with the family in the original central part of the Double T ranch house, where Tate and Molly and their twins made their home. After dinner, Tucker and Tate relaxed over a couple of snifters of good brandy while Molly went up to nurse the babies. Then the brothers joined her for the important job of putting the twins to bed.

There were baths first, followed by the intricate process of getting little feet and arms into clean diapers and snap-on sleeping shirts. Then came the singing. Tate and Molly sang their children a number of lullabies, Molly in her clear alto, Tate in his slightly off-key baritone.

Tucker, who thoroughly enjoyed his role of new uncle, chimed in on the songs where he remembered the words. He liked this whole family-life thing. A lot. As far as he was concerned, it was the smartest move his big brother had ever made, to get himself hooked up with Molly O'Dare.

By eight, at last, the babies were tucked into their cribs in the darkened nursery, their nanny watching over them from the small bedroom across the hall.

Tate announced what he usually announced about that time in the evening. "Got a few things to tie up downstairs." Tucker's brother had a study on the first floor at the front of the house. Tate kept close tabs on the family holdings at the big computer in there.

Molly moved into the circle of her husband's arms for a fond, quick kiss and then Tate headed for the main staircase.

Tucker saw his opportunity and seized it. "Got a moment?"

Molly shrugged. "Sure. How 'bout some coffee?"

"Lead me to it." He fell in step behind her as she turned for the narrow back stairs that led to the family room and kitchen below.

At the table in the breakfast room, Molly poured him a mug of coffee, brewed herself a quick cup of herb tea and settled into the chair across from him. He watched her fiddle with her tea bag and tried to figure out how to begin.

Molly knew a lot about what went on in the Junction. She was not only the town's first female mayor, she also ran her beauty salon, Prime Cut, as a place where all the women in town could gather to talk about things that most males of the species would never dare to *think* of. At the Cut, the lives and loves of the citizens of Tate's Junction were dissected and analyzed freely and openly, with no-holds-barred.

"So what's up?" Molly set her tea bag on the edge of her saucer.

Tucker decided he might as well just come right out with it. "Tell me everything you know about Lori Lee Billingsworth."

His brother's wife watched him over the rim of her cup as she sipped her tea. With great care, she set the cup down. "Taylor. Her last name is Taylor. She was married."

"But she's a widow now."

Molly gave him a measuring look. "Lucky for you, right?"

"Molly, damn it. I could use a little help here."

Tate's wife wrapped her fingers with their long, shiny red fingernails around her teacup. "What's this about? You had one sister and now you want to make it an even pair?"

Tucker gaped—and then shook his head. "Molly. You got a mouth on you."

"So I've been told. Answer my question."

"No," he said, emphatically. "It's not like that. This has got nothing at all to do with Lena. Lena and I, well, that was a long, long time ago."

Molly wore the look of a doubting woman. She asked, each word sharp with suspicion, "Water under the bridge, is that what you're trying to tell me?"

He nodded. "Lena's happy now. She loves Dirk. And you know what? I'm nothing but happy *for* her."

"But you did love her. Once."

Had he? Tucker wasn't so sure. "I was crazy over her, yeah. But love? Hell. We were kids. She wanted a life right here, in town. She wanted for us to have that big wedding she's going to have now and settle down here at the ranch house, where she was going to pop out two or three babies and do her best to help me spend Granddaddy's money."

"You're still carrying a grudge against her."

"No," he said again, even more strongly than before. "I'm carrying no grudges. I'm telling you how it was, that's all. Lena wanted a nice life, here in town. And I wanted out. Bad. We broke up—which made it possible for both of us to get what we wanted. It would have been a disaster, Lena and me. She knows it. I know it. End of story."

Well, except for that one night....

Tucker had come home from college—where he was flunking just about every course and soon to drop out— to take Lena to her prom. The night before the dance, she'd told him it was over between them, that they wanted different things and it just wasn't working.

He'd agreed with her. He'd been thinking it was time to move on for a while by then, but he hadn't known how to tell her. Even now, he could remember the feeling of sweet relief that had flowed through him when she said she didn't want to be his girl anymore.

And then she'd told him she couldn't see any way out of the two of them going to the prom together. Tucker, figuring it was the least he could do to pay her back for handing him the freedom he'd been yearning for, had promised to take her.

That night, which he'd dreaded, ended up being pure magic.

They were breaking up and still…she wove a spell around him. He found himself long-gone in love with her, more than ever before. She knocked him out. She bowled him right over.

But now?

No. All that was over. All that was long ago. When he saw Lena now, he felt a vague sort of fondness. He *liked* her now. She was always smiling, a cheerful woman, all wrapped up in herself—but in a charming way. They were friends, though not *close* friends. When he saw her now, he found it impossible to think of her as the girl he'd held in his arms on that beautiful, unforgettable night.

Tucker leaned across the table toward his sister-in-law. "So what's the story about Brody? Lori's husband couldn't have been his father—right?"

Molly sighed—and finally started talking. "No. The boy isn't her husband's. She married the husband—a dentist, an older guy—six or seven years ago, when Brody was two or three. Word is that nobody but Lori knows who Brody's real father is."

"Except for the father himself, right?"

Molly frowned. "Maybe not."

"The kid's father doesn't even know that he's a dad?"

"Tucker, how would I know? All I know is what people say."

"And that's what I want from you. What people say…"

Molly looked down into her teacup, and then back up at him. "Rumor has it some stranger came through town at the end of Lori's senior year. Lori disappeared one night in May, in one of Heck's cars. It wasn't like her, to take off like that. You know how she was. The shy, quiet, one. Hardly dated. Heck got worried she'd been kidnapped or something. He had the police out looking for her. They found her way up at the North Fork of Cook Creek, parked right on the bank, staring out over the water, crying her little heart out. She claimed that she'd done nothing wrong—and that nothing had happened to her. She'd just driven around, that was all.

"But then, a couple of months later, when she turned up in the family way, everyone in town naturally assumed it must have happened that night she disappeared. They all figured she must have met someone, that he got her pregnant and then headed out, never to be seen or heard from again."

"And when Heck found out she was pregnant, he packed her off to San Antonio."

"That's right. And she's made herself a good life there, from what I've heard. She hardly ever comes home."

Tucker got up and poured himself another cup of coffee. As he sipped, he turned and leaned on the long jut of counter that divided the breakfast room from the kitchen.

Molly said, in that way she had that cut right through the crap, "So. You got you a yen for your old girlfriend's twin sister, Tucker? You thinkin' you might like to try convincing her to come home a little more often—even to *stay* home?"

Tucker didn't answer. There was no need. He could see in Molly's eyes that she knew he did.

And he was.

"Daddy makes you crazy, huh?" Lena lay sprawled face-up on the bed in the upstairs room that had been Lori's when they were growing up.

It was after dinner. Everyone else was downstairs watching Sunday night TV. Lena had hung around before going home to her cute little apartment on Oak Street. She'd wanted some one-on-one time with Lori.

Lori dropped to the side of the bed. "Yeah. Daddy does get to me. Sometimes. Like when he tries to override me with Brody."

Lena kicked off her shoes and scooted farther up onto the mattress, grabbing a pillow and tucking it under her head. "You just never did accept the fact that you have to use your feminine wiles on Daddy."

"Feminine wiles?" Lori made a gagging sound.

Lena giggled and slapped her lightly on the knee. "Stop that. There's nothin' the least wrong with a woman using what the good Lord gave her to smooth the way with the men in her life."

"I am going to wisely withhold comment on that one."

Lena rolled to her side and studied her sister. "I still can't believe you went red—red."

Lori smoothed a hand over her own hair. "Yeah. I kind of like it."

Lena nodded. "Me, too. It looks real good."

Lori made a threatening face. "Don't you dare even consider going red, too."

"But if it looks that good on you, just think how incredible it's going to look on me."

They both laughed at that one. And then Lori said, "Hey. Go for it."

"I might. I just might…" Lena let out a long sigh, rolled to her back again and gazed up at the light fixture overhead. "Tucker was givin' you looks today at the diner." She rolled her head to face Lori again. "Don't even try to tell me you didn't notice."

Lori had no idea what to say—and her pulse was racing, her stomach drawing into knots, the way it had been doing since she first ran into Tucker yesterday at the Gas 'n Go…

Lena said, "Amazing."

"What is?"

"Oh, just the way life can go sometimes." She lifted her right hand and studied her manicure. "Tucker's interested. Really interested. In you. I could tell."

Lori tried a little teasing, hoping that would lead the subject elsewhere. "I'm surprised you noticed. You've got eyes only for Dirk."

"It's true." Lena raised both arms in a lazy stretch. "Dirk is the center of my world and I couldn't be happier about that." She let her arms flutter down and folded her hands on her stomach. "But at the same time, true love has made me more observant. And since Tucker moved back to town, I've made it a point, I truly have, to make amends for the tacky way I treated him—you know, back when. Last winter, when Dirk decided to change his will to leave everything to me, I took him to Hogan and Bravo and had Tucker do the work. Tucker is Dirk's and my own personal family attorney now and I like to think that he and I have become friends."

"Good for you," Lori said, for lack of anything better, hoping they could now leave the subject of Tucker Bravo behind.

But no. "You haven't said what you think. About you and Tucker."

"I don't *think* anything. I haven't seen him for years and years. I hardly know the guy."

"Lori. Come *on*. I mean, it seemed to me by the way you looked at him at the diner that you maybe kind of like him, too—and don't give me that huffy look. Okay, he was my boyfriend. But that was *centuries* ago. And it was pure puppy love, anyway. I know that now. It was nothing like I have with Dirk—and it's not like I *slept* with Tucker or anything. I mean, that might be kind of icky. To think of you getting together with some guy I'd seen naked, but—"

"Lena."

"Um?"

"That is altogether more information than I need to have."

Lena gave her another light slap on the thigh. "Oh, come on. I know what you're doin'. Acting all snooty to push me away. You're just too…private. You always have been. Even for me, it's tough to get through. And, as your twin, I should be the one who understands how your mind works. Lori Lee, you need to…open up a little."

"Thank you for the input."

"Oh, now, don't go getting snippy on me. Look in your heart. You'll see that what I'm telling you is true. And I *miss* you, gosh darn it. We don't see you often enough. It's like, since all that mess eleven years ago, you never want to come home." What could Lori say to that? Not much, since it was true. Lena went on. "I swear, sometimes I think if Mama and I didn't call you all the time, if we didn't keep you up-to-date on what's going on in town and stay on you until you come home now and then, we'd never see you at all."

Lori caught her sister's hand and twined their fingers together. "I know. I don't visit often enough." She said the words gently—and silently promised herself she'd make more of an effort to keep up the bond with her family.

Lena heaved a huge sigh. "You know what?" Lori squeezed her hand to let her know she was listening. "I never did apologize to Tucker about prom night. Did you?"

Lori blinked and felt her stomach squeezing tight all over again. She pulled her hand free of her sister's. "I…when would I have done that?"

"Relax. I was just asking. And think about it. The poor man still believes he went to that prom with *me*. I mean, it's not that big a deal, but still, one of these days one of us ought to tell him. When I look back on that night, I sometimes wonder what could possibly have been going through my mind, to do that to him."

Lori remembered what had been going through Lena's mind. She remembered with crystal clarity. Lena had told her. "You were mad. You were really steamed. You came home after breaking up with Tucker and you marched right up here to my room and shut the door and burst into tears. You said how you knew, you could tell, that Tucker was relieved to be getting rid of you. You said sometimes you hated being so perfect, you hated how everyone expected you to be so darn happy all the time. You said you almost wished *you* could be the mousy, shifty, shy one instead of me, how maybe then, folks wouldn't expect so much of you."

Lena gasped. "How *rude*. I didn't."

Lori nodded. "You did. Then you said you didn't know how you were going to get through prom with a smile on your face, when all you really wanted to do was to scream and stomp your feet and tell Tucker off good and proper for not loving you enough to make you his bride and settle down in the Junction with you to live happily ever after. You said you were just sick. That you were just aching to stay home and watch old movies and eat a barrel of popcorn and have yourself a good long cry."

Lena made a low sound in her throat. "Well, now you say all that, I kind of do remember—and then *you* said how *you'd* like to go to prom…"

Lori's date, a friend, a fellow biology student, had come down with mono and had to beg off. And then there was the fact that Lori had had a secret crush on Tucker since long before he and Lena had started going out.

Lena smiled a musing smile. "Yeah. Once you said how much you'd like to go to prom, things kind of took their natural course, now didn't they?" She giggled. "I'm still amazed at how well we pulled it off."

Lori had to agree on that point. "Me, too." For twins who'd always claimed they weren't joined at the hip like most identicals, it was surprising how easily they'd each slipped into the other's skin.

Lena said, "Even Daddy and Mama were fooled. Remember Daddy, snapping away, taking all those pictures of you in *my* dress, telling you how beautiful you looked, thinking the whole time he was talking to me?"

Lori couldn't help grinning at the memory. "And you spent the night dragging around in my pajamas…"

Lena giggled some more. "Mama kept checking on me. She'd say, 'Lori, sweetie, it's not the end of the world to miss your prom.' And then I'd let a few tears dribble down my cheeks and hang my head the way you used to do, all pitiful-like, and whisper, 'Mama. Please. I'd prefer to be alone.' And then *you,* what do you know? You went and got yourself crowned prom queen."

"No. I got *you* crowned prom queen."

Lena pretended to scowl. "I have to admit, I was just a teensy bit jealous when I learned I won—and I wasn't even there to get that rhinestone crown on my head."

"You? Jealous? Never."

"And then you came home so late. It was practically dawn. I was pretty darn put out with you about that—about you going out with *my* boyfriend and having such a fine old time, you didn't want to come home."

Lori felt a deep and awful stillness within herself then—the stillness that came with telling too many lies, with spending too many years waiting for those lies to catch up with her. She'd been vague that night—or rather, that morning. She'd told Lena that she and Tucker had gone out for breakfast. Since Lena would never in a thousand lifetimes have imagined that Lori would go to a motel with Tucker, the lie had worked. Lena never questioned it.

Lena said, "It was a crazy time, wasn't it?"

"Oh, yeah. It sure was." The night with Tucker had been like a world apart, the one special, enchanted evening when, at last, her every dream of being Tucker's girl came true. And then she'd come home and looked at her twin and it hit her like a safe dropped on her from a tenth-story window: she'd betrayed her own sister. Even if Lena and Tucker *were* going their separate ways, it still felt to Lori like a line she'd had no right to cross.

But she *had* crossed it. And from that morning on, things only got worse. Tucker came to the door to beg Lena to take him back—because of the night before, Lori knew it.

Lena sent him away and told Lori, "It's the best thing. And he knows it, too."

By the next night, with all the turmoil inside her over the forbidden things she'd done and the lies she'd told everyone to cover those forbidden things up, she was a complete wreck.

"And then, the next night," Lena said, eerily echoing the direction of Lori's thoughts, "you took Daddy's car and, *pouf,* you just disappeared." Lena sent her a reproachful look. "You never did tell me what happened, with Brody's dad that night. You never told me how you met him, how you—"

Lori put up a hand. "I can't. Not right yet."

That was another promise Lori had made herself. She was going to tell Lena the whole truth, too. But it only seemed right that she should tell Tucker first. Just as it only seemed right to wait until after the wedding to break the news to Tucker.

The wedding meant so much to Lena. If word got out beforehand that Tucker Bravo was Brody's father, there was going to be talk. A lot of it. Lena's big day would be thoroughly overshadowed.

Lori refused to let that happen. Tucker had gone all these years not knowing he was a dad. What difference could it make if he waited two weeks more?

"Did you hear yourself?" Lena let out a whoop. "You just said, not right *yet*. Lori darlin', I do believe this is progress. Always before, you refused to tell me, period."

"Well, I am working up to it."

Lena gave her a full-out, blinding sunny smile. "Oh, Lori. It's about time."

Tuesday, purely by accident again, Lori met up with Tucker on Center Street, in front of his law office. They exchanged greetings and he asked her how she was enjoying her visit to town.

"I'm having a great time," she told him. "Just great." And before he could ask her another question, she glanced at her watch. "Oh. I really am running so late." Late for exactly nothing—but he didn't have to know that. "I have to get going." She zapped him with a too-bright, fake smile.

"See you later, then."

"Yes. See you…" And she hurried on by.

She couldn't believe it. She'd run into Tucker four times in her four days in town.

It was beginning to feel as if fate itself were taking

a hand here. As if her own guilt and cowardice were conspiring to throw him in her path at every possible opportunity—maybe to give her the chance to say what needed saying.

Well, too bad for fate. She would tell him when she planned to tell him—in two weeks, after the wedding—and not a day earlier.

Wednesday, Lori and Lena and Brody spent a lazy afternoon out at nearby Longhorn Lake. Lori watched her son play in the sun at the edge of the water and knew the day of reckoning was swiftly approaching.

How much time was Tucker going to want with Brody? Would she and Tucker end up in an ugly custody battle? How would Brody deal with finally learning who his natural father was.

Those questions, and the thousand more that haunted her, wouldn't be answered until she talked to Tucker. And that wasn't going to happen until after the wedding.

Lori decided she'd put all thoughts of Tucker out of her mind.

For now.

There was no point in second-guessing. The moment of truth would be on her soon enough. And after that, she'd get plenty of answers—whether she wanted them or not.

Thursday morning, as Lori lingered alone in her mother's kitchen enjoying a second cup of coffee, the phone rang. She snatched the cordless handset off the wall without giving it a second thought. "Hello?"

"Just the woman I wanted to talk to."

Her mind went totally blank. "I…uh, Tucker?"

"That's right. And this *is* Lori, isn't it?"

"Uh. Right. It's me."

He chuckled. The sound terrified her. What was he after? Why was he calling? She clutched the mouthpiece in a white-knuckled grip and resisted the urge to shout into the mouthpiece: *Not now! Go away! I will talk to you—soon. Very soon....*

The frantic, fearful thoughts tumbled over each other inside her head—and then spun to a stop.

She had a moment of terrible, absolute clarity.

How many ways were there to say *coward?* At that moment, Lori Lee Taylor knew them all—she *was* them all.

Gutless. Yellow. Gun-shy with cold feet. Lacking a backbone. Weak-kneed. Lily-livered. Scaredy-cat. Big baby. Chicken...

The list went on and on. And every word in it had her name on it.

If she wasn't going to tell him until after the wedding, so be it. That didn't mean she had to jump like a spooked rabbit every time she saw his face or heard his voice.

The man was her child's father. In the end—which was coming up very soon now—she was going to have to learn to deal with him.

When she did tell him the truth, she didn't want him thinking back on how she'd run away shaking every time he came near. He wasn't going to be happy with her, when he found out. But until then, the least she could do was to treat him with courtesy and carry herself with a little damn dignity.

"I was wondering," he said. She thought, Omigod, he's going to ask me out. And then he did. More or less.

"How about you and Brody coming on out to the ranch tonight? For barbecue. Brody can play with Fargo. And out at the stables, we've got a real sweet, mild-mannered pony he might like to try riding. I'll make it my business to see he has a good time."

Lori felt that awful stillness again, the one with the weight of all her lies carried in it. How had he known to make Brody the focus of his invitation? Was it possible he'd somehow guessed the truth? Her heart lurched in a sick, rough way.

But no. Nobody knew. Except Henry. She had told him, and only him, before they were married.

Only Henry knew. And Henry was gone.

So why did Tucker make it seem like it was all about Brody?

She knew why.

She was a single mom. And if a man wanted to get close to her, he had to make it clear he understood that Brody was a big part of her life—and would be a big part of the life of any man she took seriously.

Lori shut her eyes and drew in a long, slow breath.

"Lori. You still with me?"

"Uh. Yes. Yes, I'm right here."

"So, what do you say?"

She swallowed and dared to ask, "It's all about Brody, huh?"

He laughed then. "Well, not quite all. There's also you…and me." Something within her warmed and softened at those words. And she remembered…

His lean arms around her as they danced the last dance that fateful night, his voice a velvet whisper in her ear…

"I don't want tonight to end…."

She had sighed and snuggled closer, her—Lena's—pink satin gown rustling softly against the dark fabric of his tuxedo. And then she'd lifted her head from the cradle of his shoulder, tipping her face up to show him the yearning in her eyes. "I don't either, Tucker. I want tonight to last forever…"

He looked down at her, his dark eyes shining with desire—for *her*, for *Lori*, though he didn't even know it. "We could…go somewhere. Be alone. Just you and me…"

She lowered her lashes, rested her head once more against his shoulder, felt the hungry beating of his heart beneath her ear and the answering clamor of her own.

"Lena…" he whispered, breaking her pounding heart into a thousand tiny pieces.

And still, she dared to lift her head again and smile up at him. "Yes. Let's do that. Let's go somewhere…"

"Lori?" Tucker's deep voice came to her—on the phone, now, today. "Will you come to the ranch, around five, you and Brody?"

She should tell him the truth, now.

Or tell him no.

She knew that.

Still, she opened her mouth and said, "Yes. We'll come."

Chapter Three

"Come on Fargo, come on, boy!"

Brody hauled himself out of the pool and took off, wet feet slapping the tiles, until he reached the expanse of green, green lawn. The lawn rolled out to the thick circle of oaks and pecan trees rimming the backyard grounds of the sprawling Double T ranch house. Brody ran on, across the jewel-green grass, dripping pool water, laughing. Fargo, yipping in excitement, chased at his heels.

Beyond the crown of trees, the sun had already set. Lori and Tucker sat by the pool in the gathering twilight as the boy and the dog played on the grass.

"I think he's had a real good time," said Tucker.

She slanted him a grin and took a sip from her margarita. "Understatement of the decade. He loved riding that pony. And I swear he ate a whole slab of those in-credible ribs you served up."

"I can't take credit for the ribs. They're Miranda's specialty." Miranda Coutera was the Double T's house-keeper. Tucker lifted his margarita glass. "Likewise the margaritas."

Lori tapped his glass with hers. "Here's to Miranda."

"Miranda," he echoed softly.

The pool lights came on and cast a soft glow up to-ward the wide, slowly darkening Texas sky. A pesky mosquito buzzed near Lori's ear.

She gave her neck a good, sharp slap. Then she laughed. "A summer night in Texas. Nothing like it."

"Hey. At least it's not a hundred and ten and so hu-mid you work up a sweat just sitting still." His eyes gleamed at her through the shadows. "Yet."

They shared a long glance—a little *too* long. She cleared her throat. "I do like that about San Antonio. It's not quite so humid as it can get around here."

"You never mentioned the kind of work you do there—or do you have your hands full just being a mom?"

"I'm a dental assistant. Or I was. It's a two-year de-gree. My dad paid my tuition and I went to school, start-ing right after Brody was born."

"I think somebody told me your husband was a dentist…"

She nodded. "I met Henry when he hired me for my first job. The last five years, I haven't practiced. I ran my husband's office. And it turned out I had a knack for the business end of things. I'm a good manager and I've got a talent for investing." The truth was that she'd tripled their assets in the years she and Henry were married. "I sold my husband's practice when he became too ill to work. So except for managing my investments, I guess you could say I'm between jobs."

"You're free, then," he said quietly. "To go wherever you want to go…"

He was right, she supposed. She *was* free. Not that she had any plans to move. She liked San Antonio and she'd been happy there.

And it was getting dark. Time to say goodbye. She set down her glass. "You know, it *is* getting kind of late and—"

He cut her off by picking up the spray bottle on the table in front of them. "Try this. All natural. Citronella or something. You become invisible—to mosquitoes, anyway."

"But I really think we should—"

"Come on. Give it a try."

She glanced out over the grass where Brody lay on his back, laughing in delight, as Fargo wiggled all over him, trying to lick his face. And when she looked at the man beside her again, she found herself reaching out, taking the spray bottle—and using extra, special care not to let her fingers touch his in passing. "Thank you."

"My pleasure—spray your ankles, too. Mosquitoes just love a nice, tasty ankle." She dutifully scooted her chair out enough to give her ankles and her bare thighs a couple of good squirts. That handled, she scooted in again and sprayed her arms, then lifted her hair to spray her neck. When she set the bottle on the table again, he asked, his voice low and a little bit husky, "Better?"

"So far, so good." She glanced over, saw the look of admiration in his eyes and felt underdressed in her modest tank-style swimsuit and simple button-front cover-up. She also couldn't deny the thrill of pleasure that went shooting through her—that he was looking. That he liked what he saw.

Oh, she really should go....

Tucker sat back in his chair and rested his elbows on the wrought-iron arms. "Hungry mosquitoes or not, it's damn beautiful out here." He stared off, past Brody and Fargo, toward the shadowed rim of trees.

Get up and get out, she thought. But she didn't. She studied his strong profile for a moment, thinking how handsome he was, then followed his gaze to the trees and beyond, out into the wide, clear Texas sky. A glow of orange and purple still lingered, the last of a glorious swiftly fading sunset. "Beautiful. Yes..."

"You know, I've seen the coral gardens off Bora Bora. I've climbed the Eiffel Tower, stood at the foot of the Sphinx. But I never could see the beauty of my own damn backyard—not when I was a kid, anyway."

She knew why; most folks in town did. She turned her gaze to him again. "Because of Ol' Tuck, right?" Ol' Tuck was Tucker's grandfather, Tucker Tate IV.

Tucker grunted. "Granddaddy and I were born *not* to get along." Tucker's grandfather had been famous for his hardheadedness, both in business and with his family. He'd ruled the Double T ranch house with an iron hand.

"Your grandfather was a tough one," Lori said.

Tucker shrugged. "He was always pretty good to

Tate, in his own overbearing, ornery way. But he never did much care for me."

She had to actively resist the urge to reach out and press a reassuring hand on his hard, tanned arm. The battles between Tucker and his grandfather were the next thing to legend in Tate's Junction. Tucker was constantly making the mistake of standing up to Ol' Tuck. Nobody did that and got away with it.

Tucker said, "He always believed I was the result of my mother's affair with some stranger. That got to him, that he had to raise his flighty daughter's illegitimate son and pretend I *wasn't* what he knew damn well I was. Hah. Fooled him—or I would have, if he wasn't already gone when we learned the truth." Tucker's grandfather had died three or four years ago. The truth about Tucker's father had only been discovered last summer. Tucker added, grinning, "I'm no more a bastard than my brother is—meaning, if I am, then Tate is, too."

Bastard, Lori thought. It was an ugly word. One that had little meaning, really, not anymore. Except to hidebound traditionalists, like Ol' Tuck. And Heck Billingsworth...

Tucker continued, "As far as we can figure out, our father married more than once. Who he married first is a question yet to be answered."

Lori wasn't listening. She looked out at her son rolling around on the lawn and reminded herself that he was a great kid, that she'd done the best she could and that judging by the way Brody was turning out, the best she could do was pretty damn good.

Tucker must have picked up the direction of her

thoughts, because he said, "Sorry. No offense meant, I promise you..."

It was one of those moments—and there had been several during the evening—when she could have led right up to telling him that Brody was his son. She opened her mouth. And lied some more, by omission. "No offense taken. Honestly."

He looked at her—a deep look. "Sure?" She nodded. He said, "And here I am, yammering on, just assuming that your mother or Lena filled you in on all this when we found out about Blake Bravo last year."

Lori *had* heard all about it. Her mother and her sister had taken turns on the phone with her, both of them thrilled to have such a great story to tell her. "Lena did tell me. Mama mentioned it, too. And yes, I heard that the news had everyone talking."

The story went that *the* Blake Bravo, notorious kidnapper of his own brother's son, was also Tate's and Tucker's father. Blake was supposed to have died right after Tate was conceived, but he didn't die then. He lived for over thirty more years, making his home in Oklahoma all that time. As it turned out, Blake *was* the man that Penelope Tate Bravo had run off with when she got pregnant with Tucker.

"Imagine," said Tucker, dark eyes shining now, "I've got family I didn't know I had and I've got them all over the place. A bunch of Bravo cousins in Wyoming, and one down in the Hill Country—she's married to a veterinarian. I've got half brothers in Nevada and another one, Marsh, up in Norman, Oklahoma. There are two cousins—sisters—and their families, in Northern California. And then there's the most famous branch of the family, the Los Angeles Bravos. They're richer than *we* are, which is pretty damn rich, you can take my word for it. And let's not forget Dekker, the notorious Bravo Baby, the one my dear, doubly departed daddy kidnapped all those years ago. Dekker's in his thirties now, a private investigator up in Oklahoma City."

"That's a lot of family," she agreed.

"And it's not all, believe me, not by a long shot. I have a great-uncle, James, who had seven sons. And Blake had more children. Tate and I and our half brother, Marsh, are almost certain of that." He looked so pleased with himself.

She found his enthusiasm contagious. "You love it," she said, grinning along with him, the nagging truth she hadn't told him almost—though never completely— forgotten. "You love having all that family."

"I do," he told her. "Tate had some problems with it at first, with the whole idea that the dad we never knew was a two-timing con man, and worse. But not me. It meant the damn world to me, to finally know who I really am, to know I've got people all over the good old U.S. of A. Makes me feel…I don't know. Connected, I guess. Tuned in to the real reason we're all here in the first place."

She couldn't help chuckling. "Which is?"

He tipped his head to the side—and she saw her son in him, saw Brody, saw what he would look like, when he was a man. The sight stole her breath.

And stopped her heart.

Tucker's brown-gold brows drew together. "Lori?"

He said her name and the frozen moment broke wide-open. Her heart found its rhythm. Sweet night air filled her lungs.

"Tell me," she said. It came out low, kind of breathless. And she didn't care—not right then. She didn't care that she was enjoying herself far too much, didn't care that she shouldn't do this, that the secret she kept stood firmly between them, that until she revealed the truth to him, she had no *right* to do this, no right to be sitting there, taking pleasure in his company under what could only be called false pretenses.

Right then she cared only that she *was* sitting there, beside Tucker, in the new darkness, with their son laughing out on the lawn and the pool lights making everything glow in a misty, star-dusted kind of way.

She prompted, softly, "What's the real reason we're all here?"

He canted toward her. And she found herself leaning toward him, too. He looked at her mouth and then up into her eyes. "I came back to town last year to find something—something I've been looking for my whole damn life."

"And that something was...?"

"Don't rush me," he whispered. "I'm getting there."

She made a face. "Oh, well. Excuse me."

He leaned closer still. "You're forgiven."

Warmth curled through her. "Thank you. Go on."

And he did. "It's only been in the last couple of years that I began to see that wandering the world wasn't getting me anywhere, that what I was looking for had to be right here, where I started out."

She couldn't keep herself from prompting a second time, "But what *was* it?"

One side of his mouth lifted. "You really want to know, huh?"

Did she? She wasn't sure. Still, she nodded.

And he said, "I didn't have the slightest idea."

"Wait a minute. Let me get this straight. You came back home to look for something—but you didn't know what it was."

"You got it. I only knew that *if* I came home, I would find it at last."

"And you knew this, how?"

"Lori. It's *that* I knew, not how."

"Ah. One of life's deep mysteries, then?"

"Exactly."

"You just *knew.*"

"That's right."

"And did you find *it?* Whatever it is?"

"That's an excellent question."

"Well, duh."

He laughed, then grew more serious. "It's meant so much to me, settling in at my granddaddy's big old house, finding out who I really am, learning of all the family I've got…" The words trailed off. He slowly shook his head and he looked at her in that soft, admiring way, his gaze moving from her eyes to her nose to her mouth to her chin, then back up to meet her eyes again.

Another sweet thrill shivered through her. She laughed low, partly from nerves. And partly from pure feminine excitement. "You still haven't answered the main question. Did you ever find *it?*"

"Do you realize, all those years ago, when we were kids, I never really *saw* you? Right now, I find that just about impossible to believe. How could I have been such a damn blind fool?"

Through the magic of the moment, Lori finally heard warning bells.

Too far, she thought. *I've let this go way too far.*

She made herself sit back from him and reminded him carefully, "Well, um, don't forget, all those years ago there *was* Lena…"

He shook his head. "Crazy. I'm not kidding. Crazy and impossible."

She didn't dare ask what, not that time. He just might tell her. And then what would she do?

He went on, "But then, after all these years, there you were. Getting out of that silver Lexus at the Gas 'n Go. And when I saw you, I thought—"

"No." She got the word out just in time.

He blinked. But he did fall silent. His dark eyes were suddenly filled with questions—questions she knew she wasn't going to answer. Not that night, anyway.

Oh, it was too much—much too much—and she knew it. She'd let things get totally out of control. She never should have leaned so close, never should have teased him, never should have begged to know about that mysterious *something* he'd been looking for.

She had absolutely no right to hear what he'd almost said.

Not tonight. Maybe never.

Tell him the truth. Tell him Brody's his son. Do it now, a stern voice inside her head commanded.

But she refused to hear that voice. Instead, she put out a hand and warned him softly, "Don't say any more. Please."

He captured her wrist, the movement so swift, she had no chance to jerk away. For a frozen moment, they only looked at each other, a look so deep, she felt as if she was falling.

Falling...

She tensed, drawing her hand into a fist.

And then, with slow care, he brought that fist to his mouth and brushed his warm, soft lips across the top of her clenched knuckles.

Heat went rolling through her, spinning up her arm, outward and downward, melting her midsection, bringing out the goose bumps on every inch of her skin.

And then, before she could collect her scattered wits and pull away, he let her go. "Sorry," he said. "I guess I'm moving a little too fast, here."

She started to protest, to say, *It isn't that,* but stopped herself. He'd only ask, *What is it, then?* And there they'd be, back with the one thing she couldn't quite tell him. "We really do have to go. Brody!"

Out on the lawn, her son sat up. "Yeah?"

"Come on. We have to go."

"Aw, Mom..."

"I mean it. Now."

Brody rose and came toward them, dragging his feet the whole way, Fargo trotting after him. When he got to her, he let his thin shoulders slump and stuck out his cute cleft chin. "Mom." The dog plunked himself down beside the boy and looked up, ears perking hopefully.

Brody glanced down at the dog and then back up at Lori. "We're kind of busy, you know?"

"Honey, we have to get going."

Brody groaned. "Aw, Mom…"

"No whining. Go on into the pool house and change into your shorts and T-shirt."

"But, Mom, Fargo and I were just—"

She put on her sternest, most no-nonsense expression. "Get moving." The round two-sided cabana was about fifteen feet behind where she and Tucker sat, nestled among a row of brightly blooming crape myrtles. "Now." She jabbed a thumb back over her shoulder.

Brody rolled his eyes at her and groaned some more, but he did trudge on past, with Fargo trailing after him, lazily wagging his long, frizzy tail.

"Wow," said Tucker. "You're tough."

She pretended to scowl. "Yeah. So you'd better not mess with me." Lori's flowered capris and knit top were folded neatly on a bench in the women's side of the pool house, waiting for her to get in there and put them on. She braced her hands on the arms of her chair and started to rise.

Before she pushed all the way to her feet, Tucker brushed her arm with a light hand. The touch set every nerve humming. She dropped back into her chair.

He said, "I hope we can do this again."

"Yes. Well. Um, that would be nice…"

"Hey. Look at me."

She forced herself to meet those deep, dark eyes of his and told him honestly, "I had a great time—and so did Brody, in case you didn't notice."

"I noticed…"

Beyond his broad shoulder, a lightning bug blinked on and winked out, a too-brief golden glow in the night. The crickets sang from the grass.

Lori found herself thinking what she knew she shouldn't: of all that might have been—if Tucker had answered his door that day she went looking for him in Austin, if he'd stayed in one place long enough to receive one of her letters, if she'd told him the night of the prom that it wasn't Lena he was making love to, if she'd stepped forward the next morning and told him then, when he came to the door…

If, if, if.

There was no point in going there. What might have been simply *wasn't.*

She'd kept her secret. And he'd moved away. Far, far away.

She *had* tried to reach him and he hadn't been reachable.

And then there was Henry.

Henry, who had loved her in a deep and steady way. Henry, who had been just the father her son needed. She *had* loved Henry. She still did. Henry was the rock she'd built her till-then floundering life upon. She couldn't imagine what her world would be like now, if she'd never known him. With Henry, she'd come into her own as a true adult.

Tucker still watched her. His gaze tempted her…to reach for him. To lose herself.

And it came to her: a part of her resented her own powerful response to this man who was her son's natural father. Her hard-won adult self didn't trust that he still managed to stir her in exactly the way he'd stirred her as a confused and yearning seventeen-year-old girl. When she looked into Tucker's velvet-brown eyes, she felt like a kid again. As if she hadn't matured or changed one bit in the eleven years since the unforgettable night that set her life spinning onto a new and unexpected course.

The emotions—the passions—he roused in her scared her. A lot. They made her feel *less,* somehow, than she wanted and needed to be. They called into question her whole life, all her choices, between that fateful night when Brody was conceived and this moment—this moment, when she should be in the cabana putting on her clothes, but wasn't. This moment, when she couldn't seem to make herself turn away and rise from her chair.

She gave another wimpy stab at doing what she should. "I ought to get dressed."

"I know." He gave her a smile that she couldn't quite read. It seemed part male appreciation. And part something else…

Something very, very dangerous. Something intimate and tender.

That did it.

Lori jumped to her feet and headed for the cabana, achingly aware of his gaze on her back the whole way.

Tucker watched her go, and marveled…

How had this happened? How could he be so absolutely, beyond-a-shadow-of-a-doubt *sure?* He didn't know. And as he'd told her a few minutes before, *how* didn't matter anyway.

Still, it *was* amazing. He'd only known her a few short days—and no, to him, the past didn't count. All those years ago, when they were kids and he was going with Lena, he hadn't *known* Lori then. Not in any way that mattered. Not the way he knew her now.

The past, to him, was nothing. As he'd told Lori, he'd been a fool, then.

He couldn't even *see* her then. When he tried to remember her back then, he saw a shadow of a person, a quiet girl who looked like Lena.

It was all different now. He no longer saw Lena when he looked at Lori. Now, he saw *her,* Lori Lee, completely independent of her twin. And he could see *them,* already, the three of them—Tucker and Lori and Brody. He could see how it would be, see it clear as a bright Texas morning.

He saw them as a family. Saw the nights like this one that would be theirs all the time; saw their lives, his and Lori's, together, raising Brody.

And afterward, when Brody was grown up and gone, he could see just the two of them, on their own—well, unless there were more kids to raise. That would be okay with him, too.

It would *all* be okay with him, as long as he could have Lori at his side for the rest of their lives.

It was pretty strange and new for him, yes. But he was dealing with it. He was just fine with it—in spite of the fact that he'd never been the kind to see himself *with* another person. He'd known quite a few women, been involved in a number of blazing-hot affairs. The heat and the longing never lasted. He'd never expected it to.

Looking back, he wouldn't say he'd loved them and left them, exactly. He'd simply never been the kind who considered settling down. No matter how white-hot things got, he always knew the day would come when he'd be moving on.

He'd been changing, though, in the last few years. He'd put down roots in his hometown. Now, he had no problem seeing himself as a family man; he saw himself as Lori's husband and Brody's father.

And Tucker liked what he saw.

Chapter Four

"You *what?*" Tate grabbed his brandy and took a big gulp.

"I'm going to marry Lori Lee Taylor," Tucker said calmly for the second time.

They sat in Tate's study in matching leather wing chairs, boots up on the tufted ottoman between them, sipping their after-dinner brandy while Molly was busy upstairs with the babies.

Tate slanted Tucker a glance from under the dark shelf of his brow. "Does Lori Lee happen to know that you're her future husband?"

"Not yet."

Tate chewed on that for a moment, then demanded, "You even been out with her?"

"Yep. Last night she and her boy, Brody, came over. Brody rode Little Amos. Then we had barbecue and went swimming. It was great."

"Came over? Here? To the house? I didn't see her—or the boy."

"Because you weren't here. You and Molly went out last night, remember?"

Tate blustered, "I know where I went."

"You sound just like Granddaddy, you know that?"

"Don't get on me," Tate growled.

"I'm not. It was only a statement of fact."

Narrow-eyed, Tate scowled at Tucker for several seconds. Then he grunted. "Damn. Molly told me you were asking about Lori Lee, but I didn't think…" The sentence wandered off into nothing.

"You didn't think what?"

"Well, now, Tuck. It's not as if you've had time to get to know her. She's been in town, what? A few days?"

"Seven days as of tomorrow, and—"

Tate interrupted, "You've never even been alone with her, have you?"

"We were alone last night. We talked, Lori and me. We talked for hours."

"With the little boy right there the whole time."

"Brody was busy. On the pony. In the pool. Playing with Fargo."

"Okay. All right. You had one date, then."

"So?"

"Well, you have to admit this is pretty damn sudden."

Tucker shrugged. "Sudden or not, I know what I want and Lori Lee and Brody are it—and come on.

Think about how it was with you and Molly. You wanted her from the first. Don't try to tell me you didn't."

Tate shook his head. "It's not the same. I knew Molly all my life without wanting her in the least. I only really *saw* her when she made me mad and ran for mayor."

Tucker raised his snifter in a salute. "That's it. It's the same with me and Lori. I knew her all my life. And then I finally *saw* her. At the Gas 'n Go last Saturday, when she and Brody first got into town."

"All your life? You been outta town for about a third of your life. And for that matter, so has she."

"And your point is?"

"Tuck. Listen. Yeah, I finally *saw* Molly. I realized I *wanted* Molly. I wanted her bad. But marry her? No way. I didn't want to marry her until I knew she was having my baby. And I didn't realize I loved her with all my heart till even later than that."

"Well, and that's the difference between you and me, big brother. I can see what I want and know that it's love from the get-go—or that it will be, in time."

"Naw."

"Yeah."

Tate sipped more brandy, frowned as he swallowed, and waded on in to the argument again. "What I'm telling you, Tucker, is love is a process. And it appears to me that you have skipped a few steps."

"I don't agree."

"But you don't even *know* her. You can't. Not in any way that matters."

"I do know her. I knew her the minute I saw her last Saturday. She's my future wife."

Tate looked at him long and hard. "Think of all the women you've been with."

Tucker had zero interest in doing that. "Why? What about them?"

"*They* came and *you* went, now didn't you?"

"Very funny."

"I'm just trying to get you to see that you can't exactly say you've ever been the marrying kind. You don't know a whole lot about the hard work that goes into making a life with a woman."

"I've changed."

Tate considered that statement for several endless seconds. Finally, he allowed Tucker a grudging nod. "Maybe you have changed. Some."

"No. I've changed a lot."

"Still, Lori Lee's only been a widow for what? A year?"

"Yeah. So?"

"Maybe she's not ready to get married again. Maybe she loved her husband and still does. You considered that?"

He hadn't. The idea made him feel a little sick to his stomach. "She's interested. I can see it in her eyes."

"And then there's the boy to consider…"

"I told you. I *am* considering Brody."

"It's a big step, taking on a child to raise."

"I *know* it's a big step."

"And then there's whoever the hell blew through town eleven years ago and fathered that boy. You talked to Lori Lee about *him* yet?"

Tucker was forced to confess, "No, I haven't."

"Maybe you better. Maybe it would be a good idea

to talk with her about her dead husband *and* Brody's father before you go popping any important questions."

Tucker fully intended to do just that—eventually. "I don't want to rush things."

Tate threw back his big dark head and let his deep laugh roll out. "You're marryin' her, it's a done deal—but you don't want to rush things?"

Tucker shook his head and muttered, "I don't know why I'm even talking to you about this."

"Well, I do. You need a little feedback and you realize I'm the man to give it to you."

"Is that what you call this? Feedback?"

"That's right. And Lori Lee'll be headed home to… where does she live, now?"

"San Antonio."

"She'll be headed back to San Antonio in, what…?"

"I don't know. After the wedding, I guess. Unless I can get her to say yes before that."

Slowly, Tate smiled. "Better get crackin'."

Tucker grunted as he realized that Tate wasn't completely averse to his plans, after all. "You SOB. You had me worried there."

Tate gave him a level look. "I just want you to be sure you've thought this through."

"I have."

"Glad to hear it."

"Why do you sound doubtful then?"

"Listen. You want to marry Lori Lee, I say more power to you. Long as *she* wants to marry *you.*"

"She will."

Tate tipped his snifter at Tucker. "See. There, now.

That could be your problem. Don't get too cocky, you hear what I'm sayin'? A man gets too cocky and the first thing he knows, a woman feels it's her duty to pull the damn rug right out from under him."

"You're talking about you and Molly, now. Not Lori and me."

"I'm talking about all women. And all men. Women love a man who knows what he wants and goes about getting it. He just shouldn't be too sure of himself. A woman *needs* a man who can be humble when he has to."

Tucker stopped himself from rolling his eyes. "You've never been humble a day in your life, Tate."

"Oh, yeah. I have. I've been on my knees and don't you doubt it. It wasn't easy. Specially not the first time. But a man can get used to crawling now and then. For the right woman."

"I really don't think that crawling will be necessary."

Tate only shook his head and reached for the brandy bottle to pour them both another drink.

Saturday night, Lori's mother served a rib roast so tender and juicy that when Heck carved it, the meat fell right off the bone. Heck said the blessing in his usual style: short and to the point.

They started passing the potatoes, the green beans and the gravy.

Heck turned to his grandson. "So, young man. You enjoyin' your visit to Gramma and Paw-Paw's?"

Brody gulped and nodded and got busy serving himself some whipped potatoes. He was cautious around Heck. Lori wasn't sure if he'd picked that up from her, or if it was just a matter of Heck being a loud and bois-terous man and Brody not spending enough time with him to get used to his ways.

"Can't hear you when your mouth's shut," boomed Heck.

Lori plunked the bowl of green beans down without passing it. "We can sure hear *you,* Daddy. Since you shout most of the time."

Heck stiffened. He sent one of those what-did-I-say? glances at Lori's mother. Enid gave him back a sheep-ish look. Heck said, "Well, I am so sorry if I have of-fended you—again."

Brody, who'd been watching the exchange with wide eyes, chose that moment to speak up. "We went to the lake. That was fun."

Heck pasted on a great, big smile and beamed it at Brody. "Good, son. Glad to hear it."

"And day before yesterday, we went to Tucker's house. He lives on a ranch. I rode a horse named Little Amos. I swam in the pool and I played with Tucker's dog—you know, the one I told you about. Fargo's his name."

Heck leaned toward Enid at the other end of the ta-ble and spoke to her as if the two of them were alone. "They went out to the Bravo place?"

Lori's mother gave her husband a look of great pa-tience. "Heck, honey, why don't you ask Lori?"

"Yeah, Daddy. Why don't you ask me? After all, I'm sitting right here."

"Humph. Well. Ahem." Heck turned his big head Lori's way and asked with studied care, "Did you go out to the Bravo place, Lori—girl?"

She looked into his eyes, which were the same shade of blue as her own, and she knew he was trying, that he was doing his best to get along with her, to mend the fences he'd trampled so cruelly eleven years ago.

And she *was* way too hard on him, she realized that. He loved her. He'd only ever done the best he knew how for her.

It was just that every time she looked at him, she remembered him looming over her terrified pregnant seventeen-year-old self, spewing warnings. Shouting scary threats.

Who is he? By God, I will know. Who did this to you? You will tell me and I will fix him so he never does this to another innocent girl. Who is he? Lori, you tell me now. I will know who he is and I will track him down and if he's a day over eighteen, his sorry butt is headed straight to jail...

She'd cowered under the ominous weight of her father's threats, believing, as only a scared kid can believe, that if she told, her father would do exactly what he'd promised. He'd send Tucker to jail. She'd pictured that—Tucker on a chain gang because of her and her lies. Tucker, wearing those striped pajamas they wore in old prison movies; Tucker dirty and bloody and needing a shave, beating rocks with a pickaxe in the sweltering sun.

Lori still didn't know which had hurt the worst: the threats and the yelling when she was so frightened already of what was going to happen to her—or that he had packed her off to San Antonio where he wouldn't have to watch his unmarried little girl get big with a baby and embarrass him in front of the whole town.

But that was then, she reminded herself.

Right now, she was a grown woman who ran her own life. Right now, all Heck had done was to ask her a civil question.

"Yes, Daddy. We went out to the Double T Thursday night. Tucker invited us. We had a great time."

"Well, now," said Heck. "That's nice. Real nice." She could see the question in his eyes: *Something going on between you and Tucker Bravo?*

But he didn't ask it. For once, Heck kept his peace.

Lori was grateful to him for that. She was also shamefully aware that it wasn't so much a question Heck had no right to ask, but more one she didn't want to answer.

Because of the secret she'd kept for so long.

The secret…

Funny. At home in San Antonio, where she was a respected widow whose bright son went to a good school, she'd gotten so she hardly ever thought about the secret anymore. But now that she was back in Tate's Junction, the secret just never seemed to leave her alone.

The secret was a big problem. She did know that. It was an enormous weight on her mind and heart. It wore her down. She had to get rid of it, for good and all.

And she would.

Right after the wedding.

She gave her dad a careful smile. He reached over and patted her hand. "Now, how 'bout you go ahead and pass those green beans this way, honey?" She lifted the bowl and handed it to him. "Thank you," he said.

"You're welcome, Daddy."

The next day, Lori saw Tucker at church again. And at the diner afterward. He kept catching her eye. Her pulse would race and her palms would sweat—and she would smile and nod and look away.

Later in the afternoon, Lori and her mom and sister were sitting at the kitchen table poring over fabric sample books, discussing window treatments for the new house Lena and Dirk would move into as soon as they returned from their honeymoon. The phone rang and Lori jumped. She knew it would be *him*.

Her mother turned in her chair and snared the receiver off the wall behind her as Lori actively resisted the compulsion to shriek, *Don't answer that!*

"Why, hello Tucker." Enid actually wiggled her eyebrows at Lori—as Lena jabbed an elbow in Lori's ribs.

"Hey!" Lori grumbled. Her sister only giggled—and wiggled her own eyebrows. Lori wanted to grab one of the fabric sample books and bop her twin on the head with it.

"Well, as it so happens," Lori's mother cooed into the phone. "She's sitting right here. Hold on." Enid covered the mouthpiece and shoved it at Lori. "Tucker," she whispered dramatically, as if Lori didn't already know.

Lori took the phone. "Hello, Tucker."

"Hey." His voice, so warm and deep, made her want to burst into tears. What was that old saying about liars weaving a tangled web? Oh, they did. They truly did. Lori felt the thick, many-layered web of her own dishonesty pulling tight around her, cutting off her air. He added, "I had a great time the other night…"

"Me, too," she heard herself saying. It was the truth—just not *all* the truth. "Thanks again."

"Any time—like, say, tonight? I'll pick you up at six. We can drive into Abilene. I know a great little Mexican place there."

"Tonight?" Dread coiled through her like a snake gathering to strike. She imagined the two of them— alone, with no interruptions.

And plenty of time to talk.

No. She couldn't do it. Couldn't be alone with him again and not tell him—or maybe, on second thought, she *could* be alone with him and not tell him. And that scared her most of all.

The other night had been bad enough, but at least then, she'd had the excuse that he and Brody were getting to know each other a little, that if even she *wanted* to tell him, it simply was not the time.

But if Brody weren't there, if it were just the two of them…

No. Bad, bad idea.

Her sister and her mother were both nodding frantically. She turned and faced the wall so she wouldn't have to look at them. "Oh, really. I'd better not." Behind her, Lena and Enid let out sharp groans of disapproval.

Tucker allowed a long beat of silence echo down the line before he repeated flatly, "Better not?"

She rushed into a totally fake reason why she couldn't go. "We have the big family Sunday dinner tonight and…" She let the excuse finish itself. It sounded so lame.

He thought so, too. She could hear it in his voice when he tried again. "How about later in the week, then? We could—"

"Tucker, I really can't."

He was silent. Way too silent. Behind her, she heard her mother and sister fluttering and fuming. She stared bleakly at the wall.

Finally, Tucker said, "I don't get it. I thought—"

She couldn't bear to hear him say it. "Listen. I wonder…"

"What?" The word was wariness personified.

It was a moment of total desperation. Oh, God. What to say next?

And right then, the idea came to her…

She knew what to do. She saw the way to lock herself in to the moment of truth. She'd set aside the time for it now. Right now.

An appointment. Yes. She'd make an appointment to tell him and she'd make it today.

"Hold on," she said to him. "I'll be right back."

"Sure," he replied, as if he wasn't sure in the least.

She punched the mute button and whirled on her hovering mother and sister. "I'm taking this in the other room," she told them in her most threatening tone.

They both put up their hands and fluttered their eyelashes to let her know they would neither of them ever presume to butt in on her life or her private conversations. She turned and left them, headed for the half-bath off the kitchen, where she shut and locked the door before punching the mute button again.

"Tucker?"

"I'm still here." He sounded like he kind of wished he wasn't. She didn't blame him in the least.

Get on with it, she thought. "I need an appointment. At your office. I need it for a week from Monday. Do you think you could fit me in then?"

A gaping moment of silence ensued. Then, at last, "Is this about a legal matter?"

"Uh. Yeah. That's right." Well, it was. Kind of. "Could you see me then? A week from Monday?"

"Lori, I have to tell you, this is pretty damn strange."

She couldn't have agreed with him more. "Will you see me? At your office?"

Another silence and then, finally, "Sure. Call my secretary and make an appointment."

"Thank you, I...Tucker?" He didn't answer. "Tucker?" About then, she realized she was talking to air.

Tucker had hung up.

"But you *like* him," argued Lena, when Lori returned to the kitchen and told them she wouldn't be going out with Tucker.

"And, honey," said her mother. "He's really settled down. Why, half the single women in town would be thrilled to go out with him."

"Then he should ask one of them—now, could we just not talk about this anymore? Please?"

"I don't understand you," said Lena. "I just never have..."

Tucker didn't understand it.

He'd thought, judging by Thursday night, that he

and Lori were on the same page. That at least she was attracted to him, that she'd be willing to see where things might go between them.

Guess not.

She wouldn't go out with him—but she wanted to discuss some damn legal issue with him. It made zero sense.

He ought to forget her.

But he didn't. Somehow, he couldn't. As Sunday faded into Monday and Monday into Tuesday, he thought about her constantly. More than once he found himself with the phone in his hand, about to dial her parents' number.

But he never did it.

What was the point? She'd made it painfully clear she didn't want to see him.

Until next Monday. In his office.

His assistant, Anna, had told him she'd called to set up the appointment, as per his instructions. He had her on his calendar in the 10:00 a.m. slot: *Lori Taylor, consultation.*

Consultation about what?

He didn't know. And that was damned unprofessional. He never scheduled appointments unless he had at least a general grasp of the potential client's problem and thought the case was one he might want to take on.

He ought to call her and tell her he needed to know what the meeting was about or he would have to cancel. But he didn't call her. He had the sinking feeling that if he called her, *she* would cancel. He'd never see her again.

Which shouldn't be such a big damn deal. It wasn't as if he'd be seeing much of her anyway. Right?

Thursday, he spotted her in the hardware store. She gave him a quick wave and turned away. Brody wasn't with her, so he didn't even get a chance to say hi to the kid.

It shouldn't mean this much, he kept thinking. He shouldn't care this much. Yeah, he'd had a powerful feeling that she was the woman for him. But clearly, she had no such feeling and it took two to get something going. Even Tucker, with his limited experience in long-term relationships, could figure that much out.

He considered talking to Tate about it. Or even Molly.

But what was there to talk about? Except for throwing him a pity party, what could Tate or Molly do for him now?

The answer was zip.

As Friday came around, he tried to tell himself he was being a complete sucker, an idiot, a hopeless yearning fool—which he was.

But even knowing that he was dragging around like a motherless calf didn't make him stop. He still wanted Lori, whether she wanted him or not, and that was a plain fact. He wanted Lori and the life he had dared to imagine he might have with her.

And if she wouldn't go out with him, well, he'd better get to work on finding a way to change her mind.

So she wouldn't date him. Yet.

Did that mean he had to give up and go away mad?

Hell, no.

He had to be more…understanding. He had to keep in mind that she was a widow, that she'd lost a husband.

And not only that. He had to consider how tough it must have been on her, to have had Brody all on her own at barely eighteen.

He had to accept that her trust must be gained. She'd had a rough time and she'd been hurt—by some rotten fly-by-night bastard who'd left her pregnant to fend for herself, and by the recent death of her husband.

The man who would win her would have to be patient with her.

Yeah. He had to take it slow and easy. Because he was ready. He, Tucker Bravo, was willing at last to put in the time and effort and tender care to get close to the right woman.

So she wouldn't date him. Well, then, he'd just have to find other ways to get close to her.

For instance, Lena's wedding.

He had an invitation. Lena, in her ongoing effort to show him she'd let bygones be bygones, had made sure he received one. Since half the town would be there, it was one of those events that an up-and-coming local attorney shouldn't miss.

And Tucker didn't plan to miss it.

Uh-uh. He wouldn't miss it for the world.

Chapter Five

Lena's wedding day dawned bright and sunny. The weather report called for thunderstorms later in the day. But Lena, blue eyes shining, declared that no icky bad weather would dare come and ruin the most beautiful, important day of her life.

The ceremony took place at the Billingsworth family church—the Church of the Way of Our Lord, to be specific—with Pastor Partridge presiding. The guests oohed and ahhed at the sight of the sanctuary, where lilies and roses, festooned with ivy and white satin ribbon, dripped from every available surface. More flowers stood in tall vases along the aisles and at the altar.

The place was packed. By the time the first familiar

chords of the wedding march filled the air, it was standing room only.

Lena's three flower girls, in green satin dresses, hair braided with ribbons and rosebuds, strolled down the white satin carpet that had been rolled out by two of the groomsmen before the wedding march began. All three little girls wore adorable shy smiles and carried ribbon-bedecked baskets full of pink and green silk petals. They cast the petals out along the satin aisle as they went.

Next were Lena's lifelong girlfriends, her bridesmaids and matrons, all eight of them in shimmering celery-green silk, each with a bouquet of pale pink roses and Peruvian lilies.

Lori, as matron of honor, followed the bridesmaids. Her gown was blush-pink, her flowers white roses tipped with green, threaded with green ribbon and ivy, rimmed in green lace. About five slow steps toward the groomsmen waiting at the altar, she made the mistake of glancing slightly to the right.

And there he was. Tucker. In the sixth row, with Tate and Molly.

Tucker caught Lori's eye and held it. She almost stumbled.

But she recovered just in time. She pulled her shoulders back, set her gaze firmly front where it belonged and continued her slow, stately progress toward the altar.

The best man took her hand and guided her to her spot at his side and then, with all the bridal attendants in place, the music swelled louder and Lena appeared in a long-waisted snow-white gown sewn all over with seed pearls. She carried a cascade of white Casablanca lilies, gardenias, freesias and roses twined with faux pearls and heart-shaped ivy. At the sight of her, a long, admiring sigh seemed to rise from every throat.

It was Lena's shining moment and she knew what to do with it. Through the white froth of her veil, she had eyes only for Dirk as she proceeded along the satin-carpeted, petal-strewn aisle. When she reached her groom at last, she handed her huge, trailing bouquet to Lori and she and Dirk turned to face Pastor Partridge.

The sacred exchange of vows began. Dirk faltered once or twice. A fast talker as a rule, he seemed struck speechless by the moment. Lena's voice was strong and clear and never wavered.

Lori's thoughts, there at the altar with her sister's wedding flowers in her hands, were not easy ones.

All her life, Lori had judged her twin and found Lena lacking. Deep down, Lori had considered herself superior to Lena in the ways that really mattered. To Lori's eyes, Lena, with her bright smiles and charming ways, only skimmed the surface of life. Lori, the quiet one, the straight-A student, had seen herself as thoughtful, as the one with real depth.

Now, today, standing there at the altar, Lori faced a hard truth: Lena was the better woman. Lena had waited for just the right guy. And when she found him, she never hesitated. She set about proudly and joyfully binding her life with his. Lena might have a selfish side, but she was also open and aboveboard about what she wanted and where she was headed.

Lori, on the other hand, had yet to even manage to tell her child's father that he was a dad.

In spite of her determination not to look in his direction, her gaze shifted again to Tucker in the sixth row. His eyes were waiting. Full of heat and hope.

And promises, too.

Dear God. The way he looked at her...

Like Dirk looked at Lena. Like Tate looked at Molly. As if she, Lori, was the only woman in the world.

Incredible. Her dream of all those years ago had somehow become reality: Tucker Bravo was looking only at her.

He *saw* her now. He'd told her so, that night out by the pool. He saw her now and he was interested.

More than interested.

And, Lori admitted to herself as her sister said, "I do," *she* was more than interested, too.

It was like some fairy tale come true.

Or it might have been, if not for the secret and the tangled, suffocating web of her lies.

Black clouds boiled up to the southwest as the bride and groom ducked into the long, white limo for the ride to the Throckleford County Country Club. The promised rain was on the way.

But folks weren't all that worried about the weather. The gala reception would be held at the club, a big sit-down dinner in the main dining room and then dancing in the adjacent ballroom late into the night. A little thunderstorm or two wouldn't matter, with the festivities being held indoors.

Tucker, who had slipped out of the church ahead of everyone else, reached the clubhouse well before the other guests. He tossed his keys to the parking attendant and went straight up the wide front staircase, through the main foyer to the dining room, with its eggplant-purple walls, white woodwork and ornately framed paintings of misty country scenes.

Sometimes, looking back, Tucker felt as if he'd grown up at the club. Ol' Tuck was always dragging them out there for family dinners—dinners they shared in that very dining room—or for any number of gala events put together by his grandmother and her women friends. Tucker knew every nook and cranny of the clubhouse. He and Tate and their friends used to sneak away from the adult festivities to hide in the housekeeping closets and run up and down the main staircase in the foyer.

Lena's wedding dinner was going to be one hell of a sit-down. There were at least forty round tables set with blinding-white linen and gold-rimmed crystal and china. Down at the far end, on a raised platform, stood a lone rectangular table set for six. That one had to be for the bride and groom and their two sets of parents. Tucker took a wild guess that, as the matron of honor, Lori would be seated somewhere near that main table.

He was right. He found her place card—and Brody's to the right of it—directly in front of the dais. Then he went looking for his own place.

Ten minutes later he hit pay dirt. His seat was just about dead center among the sea of tables, with Molly and Tate to his right.

Feeling no shame at all, he snatched up his place card, carried it up front and switched it with the one on Lori's left.

If any of the scurrying serving staff noticed he was messing with the seating, they didn't call him on it. They were too busy straightening silverware and making certain the impressive floral centerpieces wouldn't block the guests' views of their dinner companions.

The switch accomplished, Tucker headed for the Cottonwood Room—the club's dim, wood-paneled lounge. He took a seat at the bar and enjoyed a Scotch and water while he waited for the arrival of the rest of the wedding party.

Tucker returned to the dining room twenty minutes later. By then, the tables were filling up fast. The big room hummed with a hundred conversations. The serving staff moved in and out between the tables, setting out bread and butter, serving champagne, Cokes and cold tea on request. From a corner of the room, a six-piece band played "It Had to Be You," keeping it low, so folks could chat.

Lori and Brody were already seated. Tucker stopped near the door from the foyer and drank in the sight of them. As he watched, Lori leaned her bright head toward Brody. Her lips moved. Brody nodded and picked up his napkin, which sat on his plate folded into the shape of a swan. He shook it out and spread it in his lap.

Tucker grinned. The kid looked cute in a suit, his brown hair all slicked down, a wild little cowlick sticking up at the crown. Tucker knew about cowlicks and what a pain they could be. He had one, too, in just about the same spot as Brody's. He had to wear his hair long or in a slight spike, as he did now, to keep it in hand.

And Lori…

Damn.

Tucker openly stared, oblivious to everything but the woman in pink, thinking how he'd never seen her look so beautiful as she did that afternoon, her sleek red hair coiled high on her head, wearing that simple, elegant dress that hugged all her curves and made her delicate skin glow.

Yeah. She did shine in pink. She had that touch of cool rose in her coloring that made it work.

She reminded him of...

He blinked.

And time itself seemed to fall away. He went spinning backward, into that May night eleven years ago.

Lena had worn pink that night. And she'd outshone every other girl at the prom. They had danced every dance. He wouldn't let any of the other guys even get near her.

That night had changed everything—or so he'd thought when it was happening. That night, though he didn't tell Lena then, he decided that he wasn't letting her break up with him, after all. That night, he didn't care in the least that the big, wide world and all the strange, exotic, mysterious places in it, would never be his to know or explore. That night, he only wanted to stay right there, in his hometown, with Lena held close in his arms...

Lena...

So strange.

He could see his younger self, looking down at her as she whirled in his arms. Lena...

Or was it?

Right now, as he pictured Lena, smiling softly, gazing up at him on that long-ago night, it wasn't Lena he saw. He was sure of it. He looked down and…

He saw Lori in his arms.

It couldn't be. It wasn't. Of course not. His mind was playing weird tricks on him, that was all.

Still, somewhere deep at the center of himself, he was certain…

Blazing heat flooded up under the collar of his silk dress shirt. The walls pressed in on him. He couldn't breathe.

And then Lori looked up from the table where she sat with Brody. She saw him.

And she smiled. Sheepishly. Hopefully.

Damn. She was beautiful.

And somehow, her smile did the trick. The world righted itself. Everything spun back into place.

The past wasn't now.

Just as Lori wasn't Lena.

He almost laughed out loud at his own idiocy. It made a strange kind of sense, he supposed—that now, with the way he felt about Lori, it would seem to him that it must have been her and not her twin he held in his arms that night.

Funny, how a man's mind could play tricks on him when his heart got involved.

And as much as that one night still haunted him now and then, as much as what had happened then didn't quite add up—as much as, when he looked back on it, he was troubled by the idea that Lena hadn't really seemed like Lena…

It simply didn't matter. It was years ago. Lena was over it and so was he. They had both moved on.

What mattered was right now. What mattered was the hopeful smile on Lori Lee's soft mouth.

Someone jostled his elbow. "'Scuse me," he said automatically, not sparing so much as a glance for whoever had bumped him. He started forward, eyes on the prize, moving swift and sure around the tables, until he reached Lori's side.

"Tucker!" Brody's face lit up in a wide smile of greeting.

He gave the boy an answering grin. "Hey, Brody. How you doing?"

"Okay." Brody stuck his finger under his collar. "'Cept for this suit." He made choking noises.

"Brody," Lori warned softly. Brody heaved a sigh and took his finger out of his collar.

Tucker winked at him. "Lookin' good, though."

"You think?" Brody stretched his neck and smoothed his kid-size tie.

"No doubt about it." Tucker dared to turn his gaze to the woman in pink. "And you…" There were no words. He said the one that came closest. "Beautiful."

Her soft mouth trembled on a radiant smile. "Why, thank you…"

He reached down and plucked the place card from the empty spot beside her. "Well, what do you know? This is my seat."

Her expression said she'd already looked at his place card. Still, she teased, "No way…"

He turned the card around so she could read his

name—just in case she hadn't already. "Yep. 'Fraid so." He pulled back the chair and slid into it, grabbing his swan-shaped napkin and shaking it out to lay it across his lap.

She leaned close. He got a whiff of her scent, a light scent, as tempting as the sight of her in that pink dress. She asked out of the side of her mouth, "Where did you put Charlie Bowline? He was here a few minutes ago. Apparently, one of the ushers told him he was seated at this table."

Tucker turned his head enough to snare her gaze. And smiled. Slowly. He watched her lips soften and part a fraction. Her eyes changed, clear blue going soft and smoky.

He said, "Mr. Charles Bowline will be sitting with Tate and Molly Bravo. If he ever manages to find his seat, I'm sure he'll have a terrific time. Tate and Molly are a lot of fun."

"Charlie *is* the best man, you know," she murmured chidingly.

"Don't say that. You'll hurt my feelings."

She pressed her lips together to keep from laughing, but still the corners of that sweet mouth trembled. "*Dirk's* best man, I mean."

"And I hope he finds his seat quickly." A waiter filled his gold-edged flute with champagne. He lifted it toward Lori. She picked hers up and they tapped them together.

"Hey. Me, too." Brody had his Coke raised high.

Tucker tapped the kid's glass and so did Lori. "To the best man, wherever he may be."

The food came—skewered shrimp and then salads

and a main course of filet mignon and stuffed baked potatoes. It was damn good, all of it. Surprising, considering the size of the crowd. In Tucker's experience, the bigger the dinner, the worse the food.

Not that the food mattered. To Tucker, the company was what counted—and since the company included Lori, all was right with the world.

They chatted with the other guests at their table—two couples from Abilene, friends of Dirk's family, and a sweet elderly lady: Dirk's great-aunt. Beyond the tall windows, the sky slowly darkened to pewter-gray as the promised storm rolled in. Not a problem. They were all safe and dry and having a great time.

Neither Tucker nor Lori mentioned the mysterious appointment she had with him Monday, or their phone conversation the previous Sunday, when she'd as good as said she'd never go out with him. By unspoken agreement, they kept things light and general.

That was okay with Tucker.

She was beside him and he saw no reason she wouldn't stay there for the rest of the afternoon—even on into the evening if he got really lucky.

There would be dancing.

Oh, yeah. He was a happy man.

Everything seemed workable, now. The afternoon and evening stretched out ahead of them. Sunday, he'd see her at church and at the diner. And Monday…well, she'd set that up herself. Whatever legal matter she wanted to discuss with him, she'd be right there in his office.

He'd have another chance to convince her of how they should be spending more time together.

Like, say, the rest of their lives.

No. He smiled to himself. He wasn't going to push her too fast. He would take it nice and easy and slow…

After the main course was cleared off, Heck Billingsworth, up at the bride's table, rose and tapped his water goblet with his fork.

"Ahem, ahem. Ladies and gents. I'd like to say a few words about how much this special day means to Enid and me…"

Brody sat patiently through several rounds of toasting. But all that sitting was a lot to ask of a ten-year-old boy. By then, the other kids in the room were either fiddling around in the doorways or disappearing into the main foyer, just like Tucker and Tate used to do at similar events when they were kids.

Brody leaned close to Lori and whispered, "Mom. Can I go play with the other kids now?"

She let him go, after getting a promise that he'd stay in the main entrance area or in the ballroom, where she could find him. "No wandering off outside. I mean it."

"I won't, Mom. I promise." And Brody was out of there before Dirk's father could rise to offer yet another toast.

A half an hour later, after everybody and his brother had taken a turn at raising a glass, Heck stood and announced that the band would be moving to the ballroom. Outside, thunder rolled and lightning blazed down from the dark belly of the clouds.

Heck let out his booming laugh. "This here's Texas, ladies and gentlemen. No puny thunderstorm is going to spoil our good time."

Answering laughter rippled through the crowd. Everyone applauded.

Tucker pushed back his chair and offered Lori his hand. "The first dance is mine."

She laid her soft hand in his.

Chapter Six

Tell him, Lori thought, for the hundredth time that evening. Tell him, *tonight*...

It was well after eight and outside, though daylight still lingered somewhere above the thick, black clouds, it seemed like it was already nighttime. The rain had started, a hard rain, pouring down. Through the row of windows that looked out on the ballroom's long veranda and the wide, curving driveway at the front of the clubhouse, lightning flared in sudden, bright flashes. Lori whirled in Tucker's arms. She looked up into his gleaming eyes as she swayed in her pink gown and she shivered at the seductive thought that somehow, time had spun backward. Somehow, that long-ago prom night was happening all over again.

It was that night again…

Only better.

This time, there was no masquerade. This time, Tucker wasn't calling her Lena. This time, he knew which twin he whirled across the floor. This time, the magic was real.

And when this song ended, she promised herself, she would lead him to some quiet corner and tell him the secret she'd kept from him for so long.

Yes, it would probably go badly.

But she couldn't lie to him—or herself—any longer. Tucker might be furious with her when he learned the truth, and rightfully so. But he wouldn't take it out on Lena and Dirk. He wouldn't ruin the party. He wasn't that kind of man and she knew he wasn't.

Yes, word would be bound to get around town eventually. But by the time that happened, Lena would at least be off on her honeymoon.

The song ended.

Lori swayed closer to Tucker. "I wonder…"

His arm tightened at her waist. He breathed in her ear, "What? Anything. Name it…"

"A few minutes. Alone…"

He chuckled. She felt the happy sound vibrate all through her. "My thoughts exactly." He let go of her waist, but not of her hand.

The next number started up as he turned. Pulling her along, he wove through the crush of dancing couples, guiding her from the floor.

They tried the main foyer first. But most of the kids were in there, fooling around on the stairs, chasing each other in and out of the seating areas. She caught sight of Brody, playing with a couple of other boys near the front desk. His little tie had come undone and his jacket was nowhere to be seen. She opened her mouth to ask him where the jacket went, but Tucker tugged her along and all she had time for was a quick wave. Brody sent her a wide, happy grin and went back to his game.

They passed through an arch into a hallway—a nice, dim one. But not empty. People strolled up and down it, going to and from the Cottonwood Room at the far end.

Courtly old Dr. Flannigan, who'd been the Billingsworth family physician for years, came striding down the hallway toward them. He smiled his crinkly warm smile at the sight of them. "Tucker. Hello. And Lori. My, my. Aren't you a vision? You and the lovely Lena, both."

"Why, thank you, Doc." She gave him a smile.

"Believe me, the pleasure is all mine."

"Hi, Doc," Tucker said—and kept going. He muttered something—probably a swear word—under his breath and turned a corner to another hallway, the one that led to the powder room and the men's room. But two women, bridesmaids, emerged from the powder room. They both called greetings.

"Hey, Lori. Tucker...."

"Great party, huh?"

"Darlene, Louisa..." Tucker saluted the two pretty women in celery-green and turned to lead Lori back the way they had come.

They tried the dining room. No go. The serving staff

was still busy in there with the big job of cleaning up after the wedding banquet.

One of the waiters asked, "May I help you, Mr. Bravo."

Tucker chuckled, a wry sound. "Not unless you can all clear out of here on the double."

The waiter frowned in bewilderment. "Clear out, Mr. Bravo?"

Tucker clapped him on the arm. "Never mind. Just a joke…"

The waiter forced a laugh. "A joke. Oh. I see…"

Tucker took pity on the poor guy. "Go ahead. Keep at it. Sorry to interrupt."

The waiter nodded and went back to loading dirty dishes into plastic crates. From the ballroom, Lori could hear her father's voice, amplified over the club's PA system. He must have taken the microphone from the wedding singer.

"And now for the big moment. Time to cut the cake…"

Tucker headed back to the ballroom, pulling Lori with him. With so many guests everywhere, private corners were in short supply.

So all right, she thought. *Now's not the right moment….*

But she wasn't giving up. She *would* tell him that night—*later* that night. She'd send Brody home with her parents and she'd go with Tucker, out to the Double T, or wherever. It didn't matter. Just as long as they went someplace where they wouldn't be disturbed.

Yes. That would be better than trying to explain everything right now, in the middle of the wedding party, anyway. Much better with just the two of them, truly alone together, somewhere there'd be no possibility of an interruption. That was how it should be, she saw that now: the two of them, alone.

Plus, she couldn't help thinking, if she waited until the party was over, she'd have another few hours of this magic with him, another few hours until the awful moment of truth....

And okay, she was only proving to herself, once again, that she was a coward in every last, sniveling sense of the word. But what could she do if there was no place for them to talk?

Nothing. Until later.

When she *would* do it. Absolutely. No backing out.

Just as she was getting used to the idea that she was off the hook for a little bit longer, they reached the ballroom.

And Tucker kept going.

He pulled her along near the back wall as the guests gathered around the stage where a green-skirted table now stood crowned with Lena's enormous five-tiered, buttercream rose-bedecked cake. Lena and Dirk and Heck were all up there and Heck was shouting about love and forever and what a lucky man Dirk was as the wedding photographer snapped away.

Tucker kept going, toward the double doors on the side wall that led out to the veranda. Which was crazy. They couldn't go out there. Beyond the windows, lightning flashed and thunder boomed and rolled away in a crashing rumble.

Lori dug in her heels. "Tucker, it's wild out there."

He hardly glanced back at her. "It's under cover. The

worst that can happen is the wind will mess up your hair...."

"Oh, Tucker..." Her heart raced and her cheeks burned and she let him continue to pull her along. Excitement and fear and anticipation swirled around inside her, a storm within to match the one outside beyond the veranda.

All at once, everything seemed to have gone crazy and wild—wild as the wind she could hear crying beyond the clubhouse walls. One of the wait staff had gone up on the stage to whisper in her father's ear. She heard Heck say, "Folks. Folks. I need everyone's attention. We have a little situa—"

She didn't hear the rest. Tucker had pushed on the bar that opened the door and they were slipping through it. The door shut itself instantly, almost catching her long skirt, which she managed to tug to safety at the last possible second.

A hard gust of wind blew down the long, deep porch, lifting her skirt and then plastering it hard against her legs. Her formerly sleek hairdo pulled loose of its pins and blew in her eyes and across her mouth.

Out past the porch roof, the rain pounded, huge drops mixed with hail. The sky in the distance lay in heavy layers of gunmetal gray. Lightning slithered down out of the clouds, slicing the grayness with its hot-white gleam. Thunder roared.

Staff members had already been out there to take in the chair and sofa cushions. The bare wicker furniture skittered around in a jerky dance, dragging against the porch boards.

Lori swiped a few strands of hair from her mouth. "Tucker, I don't know if we—"

"This way." He led her over, out of sight of the windows, into the corner where the wall of the foyer jutted out toward the wide entrance steps. He pulled her around and backed her up against the wall so she was sheltered from the wind. Then he braced a hand on the wall to either side of her, boxing her in. "Better?"

"I…" Words deserted her. She looked up at him and she knew he was going to kiss her and she also knew that she wasn't going to stop him. Still, she made a piddling little effort at it. "I think we should—"

"Shh," he whispered, as beyond the shield of his big, warm body, lightning flared in a chain of bright explosions, followed by bursts of thunder, booming, then rolling away, then booming some more. Hail drummed on the roof over their heads.

Tucker ignored the fury of the storm. He nuzzled her temple, whispered, "Lori. I swear. I was going to go slow, you know? But I don't want to go slow. I want to kiss you. Please. Say it's all right."

All right?

It was more than all right—except for the fact that she should tell him about Brody first, before they did any kissing. She should tell him about Brody, and then, if he still wanted to kiss her, they could take it from there.

But there was a problem.

She was doing that falling thing. She was dropping, drowning, melting into those velvet-brown eyes of his. The wild storm beyond the veranda, the three hundred wedding guests on the other side of the wall…

Everything—all of it—receded. The world went quiet and still. They'd entered the center of their own private storm. There was only Tucker. Tucker, who wanted to kiss her. And Lori, who only longed to kiss him right back.

She lifted her face, anticipation shivering through her like ripples on a glassy pond.

"Say yes," he whispered. *Yes.* A truly beautiful word—and, all at once, the *only* word she knew. "Yes," he prompted again.

So she said it. "Yes…"

And his lips descended.

Beyond the veranda, the rain came down in punishing sheets, the hail pounded and the lightning flared, answering claps of thunder booming out a moment afterward.

Tucker covered Lori's sweet mouth with his own— and it happened again. The driving beat of the rain, the bright bursts of lightning, the crash and roll of the thunder—all that, everything that made up the real world— faded away.

It was that night again. Eleven years ago. It was that night…

And *this* woman.

Amazing. Incredible. The warm, thrilling fit of her mouth under his…the very taste and scent of her: the same. Exactly the same. He thought, *Lori. It was Lori, that night…*

He thought it, and then he let it go.

It didn't matter, what crazy tricks his mind and his senses insisted on playing on him. *This* was what mattered.

This woman. This moment.

This perfect kiss…

He deepened the kiss, pressing himself against her, clasping her arms to pull her away from the wall enough that he could slip his hands around her and gather her close.

She shuddered and sighed and raised her slim arms to clasp his neck. He went on kissing her, tucking her into him, feeling the singing, smooth length of her all along his body, breathing her scent, hearing the rustle of that pink silk dress like a whispered promise of pleasure to come as she kissed him more deeply and pressed ever closer.

This… yes! This was all he wanted. This woman, this moment, with his arms around her…

It just didn't get any better than this. He wanted to go on kissing her forever.

But then she took her hands from around his neck and lowered them to his shoulders. Lightning flared and thunder exploded and he felt the gentle, insistent pressure as she pushed at his chest.

And he knew she was right. It was neither the time nor the place to get too carried away. He lifted his head and looked down at her flushed cheeks and tempting, kiss—swollen lips and again he had that weird, déjà vu feeling he'd been having since he saw her at the table with Brody. He gave her a smile and whispered her name. "Lori…"

"Oh, Tucker," she murmured, looking sweet and bewildered and adorably unsure. "If only…"

A hard gust of wind brought a spray of rain and hail

slanting onto the veranda. It spattered the boards at their feet and stained the hem of her dress a darker pink.

He swore at his own idiocy and grabbed her hand. "I was nuts to bring you out in this. We should get the hell inside." He started to turn.

But she held on, tugged him back. "No. Listen, I—"

"Tucker!" It was Tate's voice, from behind him. Tucker cast a glance over his shoulder. His brother was braced in the half-open door to the ballroom. "Damn it to Hell. There you are!" His usually tanned face had a grayish cast.

Tucker turned. "What's up?"

"We got a call. We're under a tornado warning. Clouds boiling up to the south, behind the clubhouse. Things don't look good. It's time to head for the cellar."

Chapter Seven

"Listen." Lori motioned for silence and huddled closer to Tucker. "Do you hear it?"

Tucker did—in the distance to the north, beyond the wind-tossed oaks that lined the wide front driveway. The storm siren in town had gone off.

Lori's face went dead white. "Oh, God. Brody…"

"Settle down," Tate advised. "So far, it's just a warning. But we'd better not fool around with it. Come on, let's go." Tate held the door for them and they ducked inside, where the ballroom was empty except for the tight line of silent, frightened-looking people snaking out from the braced-open double doors to the kitchen.

The club's manager hovered at the back of the line, herding everyone forward. At the opposite end of the room, up on the stage, Lena's wedding cake waited, alone in a spotlight, surrounded by band equipment.

Lori demanded, "Tate. Please. Brody—have you seen him?"

Tate had already rushed past them. He sent her a bleak look back over his shoulder, but he didn't break stride. "Sorry. I haven't. But we tried to send the kids down first. Come on. Get in the line."

"We have to find Brody," Lori insisted. "Brody!" she called, pulling her hand free of Tucker's, racing for the stage, as if the boy might be hiding up there, behind that big cake. When no answer came, she paused, pink skirts swaying and put her hands to her face. "Oh, God. Oh, God…"

Tucker caught up with her. "Lori." He took her by the shoulders, turned her to face him.

"No. No…" She shoved at his chest. "Let me go."

He held on. "Steady. Don't panic. Tate said he's probably safe in the basement." She stared at him, terrified, her slim body shaking. He grabbed her hand again. "Come on. We'll find out where he is."

She let him lead her. They edged through the door to the kitchen. He apologized as they went, reassuring the worried guests who'd been waiting their turn in line that they weren't trying to cut ahead.

Beyond the doors, amid the steel counters and industrial-sized appliances, Molly, Dirk and Heck had taken charge of the crowd.

"That's right, folks," said Molly, at the head of the line, near the inside wall where a door opened onto cellar steps. "Keep it calm and keep it moving."

"Easy," Dirk added. "There's room for everyone."

"Two at a time, now," Heck instructed. "No need to push."

One of the guests cried, "But there're hundreds of us!"

Another demanded, "Yeah. How can you say there'll be room?"

"No problem." Tate, who'd taken a station between Dirk and Molly, spoke up. "I've been down there. The cellar's as big as the ballroom. Lots of storage, several rooms. Plenty of space. Room for everyone…"

It looked to Tucker as if they had maybe two-thirds of the guests below ground already. The line was moving amazingly fast—because the club's manager, and Molly, Heck, Dirk and now Tate, as well, were keeping everyone calm and moving forward.

Lori pulled her hand free of Tucker's grip and rushed to her father. "Daddy, did Brody already go down there?"

Heck frowned. "I thought he was with you…"

"Mama? Lena?"

Heck looked ahead, to the front of the line. "They've gone on downstairs."

Lori spun on her heel and dashed over to Molly. "Did you see Brody go down there?"

Molly continued to wave the line of guests forward as she shook her head. "No. I don't think I've seen him. I could have missed him, but I've been watching for the kids I know…"

Right then, the lights flickered and went out. A collective gasp rose up from the people in the ever-shortening line. Shadows engulfed them, though gray light still bled through from the open doors to the ballroom.

Someone let out a low, terrified whimper. "It's happening. It's coming…"

Tate said, "It's okay, folks. There's enough light to see by. Just keep moving, nice and steady…" The line had cleared the door to the ballroom. In no time at all, they'd have everyone down the stairs.

"Oh, God…" Lori whirled for the other set of double doors, the ones that led out to the dining room.

Heck called, "Lori—girl. Wait. You've got to get—"

She didn't break stride. "I've got to find Brody…"

Heck started to follow her. "Lori!"

Tucker slid in front of him. "Watch the line. They need you. I'll look after her."

"My grandson. Dear God. We have to—"

"Don't worry. We'll find him." He said it with a lot more certainty than he felt. Damn. Who could say where the boy was now? He could already be safe underground.

But there was no stopping Lori. She was moving and moving fast. Tucker rushed to catch up with her, not waiting to hear Heck's reply.

She raced around a jut of steel counter, headed for the dining room doors. When she got there, she yanked a door open just wide enough to slide through. Tucker caught it and followed, into the deserted dining room with its now-bare tables and stacks of crated dishes.

"Brody!" Lori cried. "Brody, where are you?"

"Lori. Wait."

She ignored him. Pink skirts lifted high, she zipped under the arch that led to the foyer. "Brody! Brody!"

Impossibly, that time, there was an answer. "Mom!" The kid came running from the shadowed hallway that led to the Cottonwood Room. "What's going on? It's dark! We were playing hide-and-seek. I was *it*. I found this sweet hiding place and I waited and waited and—"

Lori was all at once calmness personified. She put up a hand. "Brody. We've got to move, now. Come on, come on." She reached out, wiggling her fingers. The boy ran to her and took her hand.

Outside, there was the strangest sound. Like a train racing toward them, bearing down.

Brody's eyes went wide as dinner plates. "What's that?"

"This way." Tucker grabbed Lori's free hand. He ran, pulling Lori who pulled Brody, past the main desk at the back wall of the reception area, down a short hall to another door, a single one, that led into the kitchen. He shoved that door open and held it, ushering Lori and Brody in ahead of him.

The sound was louder than any train by then. It roared around them, engulfing them. Glass shattered, walls of it, a series of sharp explosions, seeming to come from everywhere at once—the windows busting inward—in the dining room, the ballroom, all over the clubhouse.

The roaring, impossibly, grew even louder.

Tate stood alone at the open door to the cellar, urging them forward. "Come on, hurry up!"

And the twister was on them.

The shut doors to the dining room flew outward and blew off their hinges into the other room. Simultaneously, the doors to the ballroom banged shut and then open—twice. Then they too ripped away and blew off.

Fury engulfed them. Pots and pans and any number

of sharp objects rose and went flying. Tucker herded Lori and Brody ahead of him, fighting every inch of the way, as the whole world broke loose from its moorings and the roaring became a monster that swallowed them alive.

It was all so *slow* after that. A minute—two, maybe—stretched into an eternity of terror, of sudden hard blows and noise.

The wild monster of roaring wind lifted Brody straight up off the floor—and threw him directly at Tate. Tate, miraculously, caught him.

"Go!" Lori shouted. "Go down, now!"

Tate turned and descended, as Brody cried, "Mama!" his young hands reaching, grasping, over Tate's broad shoulder, as if he could pull Lori to safety with him by sheer effort of his ten-year-old will.

Tucker had Lori hard by the waist. He pushed her forward. Things kept hitting him—a knife handle, a wooden bowl; a dish shattered against his shoulder. It didn't hurt. None of it hurt. He felt each blow as if it had been delivered with intent. The wild monster fought him. He fought back. The monster wouldn't—couldn't—win.

The door to the cellar came off its hinges, lifted, flattened above their heads, spun like a plate, and flew out the hole where the ballroom doors had been.

Lori screamed.

He urged her onward. "Go, move, we can make it."

She surged valiantly forward, her dress plastered hard to her legs, slowing her progress—until she grabbed it and hiked it up around her waist. The dress flapped back, wrapping around him, holding on tight like a clutching, desperate living thing.

From overhead, above the ceiling, on the second floor, there was an earsplitting ripping sound. One part of Tucker's mind placed the noise: the roof must have blown off.

Tucker kept his focus, kept pushing Lori from behind, every inch toward that cellar door a triumph, a victory over the monster that roared and clattered and beat at them and threatened to tear them apart.

They made it to the door and she was just about to duck into the stairwell, when the walls started going. Within the roaring rose a groaning and a horrible, screaming, creaking sound.

Tucker staggered on the shifting floor.

Lori cried his name, "Tucker!" and turned, reaching back to grab for him. Before he could tell her to go on, to go forward, to get down the damn stairs, a white stoneware mixing bowl materialized out of the spinning chaos, flying straight at her. It struck her at the temple, breaking neatly in half, the pieces pausing in midair and then blowing off in opposite directions. Blood bloomed at her forehead, welled, spattered everywhere.

The walls were falling in on them. Platters and frying pans whizzed by them—and Lori wore the strangest, most tender, sad look.

"Sorry…" She formed the word, without sound, as the blood ran into her mouth, sprayed her pink dress and the front of his suit. "So sorry. Ruined everything…" Her eyes drooped shut beneath the curtain of blood. She fell toward him and he caught her.

Her limp body anchored him.

He was able to take that one more step, to gather her

to him, lift her high against his chest, and surge for the stairs. He went down as the ceiling gave way and came crashing to the floor.

Chapter Eight

In the shadowed candle and lantern-lit recesses beneath the clubhouse, a deep hush descended.

From above, there was silence. Terrible. Total.

The monster had moved on.

Tucker sat on the bench that a few kind souls had vacated for him when he came down the stairs with Lori limp in his arms.

She lay stretched out beside him, too pale and very still. Her bright head, matted with blood, rested in his lap. Someone had handed him a clean white bar towel. He pressed it to the wound on her temple, watching it slowly soak crimson, the dark stain spreading, absorbing the white.

He told himself the flow was slowing. But he really wasn't sure that was true.

Brody stood beside the bench holding Lori's limp hand. His young face was set, his mouth a bleak line. Lori's mother and father and Lena, Dirk at her side, hovered a few feet away, all of them silent as the quiet from above.

Someone nearby spoke into the hush. "It's over…"

And then, from aboveground, came a slow, painful creaking sound. Something fell with a shuddering crash.

"Oh, sweet Lord," a woman cried.

"What was that?" a man demanded.

No one answered him. Who the hell could say?

Tate pulled a cell phone from his inside jacket pocket. He flipped it open and gave it a try. "No go," he said. "That big boy must have knocked out a tower or two." Tate turned to the club manager. "You got a land line down here?"

Near the wall, where water had begun to trickle down from broken pipes above, one of the bridesmaids spoke up. "There's one right here." She took the receiver off the hook and put it to her ear. Then she shook her head. "Dead."

All around them, people were trying their cells—and getting nothing.

Tate said, "Okay. Let's check out our chances of digging out of here."

He chose a couple of able-bodied men to go with him up the stairs. The club's manager and two of the wait staff went the opposite direction, headed for the outside entrance, an in-ground steel door, mounted in concrete, reached by an underground corridor that ran out about ten yards from the clubhouse.

Tucker left them to it. Right then, all he cared about

was the unmoving, blood-spattered woman in his arms. No way would he leave her side. He stared down at her still face and a word burst like a bright light into his stunned mind: *doctor.*

Damn. What was wrong with him? A doctor should have been the first thing he asked for once they made it down those stairs. He glanced up. "Doc Flannigan. Where's Doc Flannigan?"

Lori's dad, shell-shocked as the rest of them, visibly shook himself. "The doc. Why the hell didn't I think of that?" Heck raised his voice to his best booming roar. "Doc! We need Doc Flannigan over here, now!"

The word went out through the cellar's warren of rooms.

"Doc Flannigan."

"Anybody seen Dr. Flannigan?"

"Doc Flannigan. They need him up front."

A couple of minutes later, the tall, white-haired gent eased his way through the crowd. When he reached the bench, his silver brows drew together. "Oh, my." He handed his jacket to Brody. "I wonder, could you hold on to this for me, young man—and move back over there just a little?"

With obvious reluctance, Brody laid his mother's hand gently on her stomach, took the jacket and stepped back. Tucker watched him, thinking what a terrific kid he was. Ten years old and holding it together with a building collapsed on top of them and his mother out cold and covered in blood.

"Thank you." The doctor sent the boy an encouraging smile as he rolled up his sleeves. He turned to Tucker. "Is she breathing normally?"

"Yeah, as far as I can see."

The doc said, patiently, "Son, with her head in your lap like that, there is some restriction of the airways…"

Calling himself ten kinds of thoughtless idiot, Tucker carefully eased out from under her, guiding her head to the bench with a cautious hand, keeping steady, gentle pressure on the wound the whole time.

The doctor moved closer. "Any other injuries—beyond this nasty head wound?"

Tucker said, "I don't think so. But stuff was flying all over up there. She might have a bruise or a cut or two."

"Nothing major, though—other than that gash on her head?"

Tucker frowned. "It was wild up there. I can't say for sure…"

"Let's have a look, why don't we?" The doctor glanced over his shoulder. "Bring that lantern close. Someone get me some clean towels, please. And something to cover her."

The man with the lantern stepped up and held it high. Two women moved off—presumably in search of the towels and a blanket.

Dr. Flannigan examined the angry, swelling gash. *Yes,* Tucker thought with a grim surge of triumph, the flow of blood really had slowed. Flannigan gently poked and prodded. He checked Lori's pulse and lifted her eyelids, one and then the other.

About then, Tate and the men returned from the stairs.

"That exit's blocked solid," Tate said, scowling. "We'll have a hell of a time digging out that way...."

Molly, who'd been hanging back near the wall, stepped close to her husband and slid her hand in his. Tucker guessed, from the look on her face, that she was thinking of their babies, hoping they were safe with the nanny in the basement at the Double T. Tate lifted their joined hands and pressed a kiss on the fingers twined so tightly with his.

The two women returned with a stack of bar towels, what looked like neatly folded tablecloths—and a bowl of water.

"Water," said the doc. "Wonderful."

One of the women spoke up. "There's a laundry room, down the hall. The sink faucet in there is still working."

"Excellent." Flannigan wet a towel. "Let's see if we can get a better look here..." He dabbed at the bloody mess over Lori's eye.

About then, the club manager elbowed his way toward them from the other direction.

Tate said, "Well?"

The manager actually dared a smile. "The outside exit is clear. We can get out, no problem. Plus, there are choppers overhead and we heard sirens. Help is definitely on the way."

The E.M.T.s came down the corridor from the outside exit to get Lori. They loaded her onto a stretcher, carried her out and put her in the ambulance. They were headed for Tate Memorial, the hospital that Ol' Tuck had generously endowed. Memorial was big enough to have state-of-the-art machinery, its own E.R. and a surgeon with a solid handle on head trauma.

Tucker insisted on riding in the ambulance. Nobody—not Heck, Enid or Lena—argued with his right to be the one to stay with her.

He spoke to Brody before he climbed into the back of the big white van. "Your mom is going to come through this just fine."

The boy looked small and lost, standing there in the darkness and the drizzling rain in front of the collapsed ruin of what had once been the clubhouse. He asked, doubt in every word, "How do you know for sure?"

Somehow, Tucker managed a grin. "Trust me. I'm not letting anything happen to her."

Brody surged forward and grabbed him around the waist, hugging him hard. "Promise?" he whispered, his nose squashed into Tucker's chest. "Promise?"

Tucker hugged him back, his own throat locking up, surprised at the strength in the young arms around him. Damn, he thought, what a kid. He coughed to clear the tightness away. "Absolutely. I swear it."

One of the E.M.T.s spoke from the bed of the open van. "Mr. Bravo. We've got to get moving."

Brody's arms dropped away. He swiped at his nose with the back of his hand.

Heck, who stood a few feet away with Enid, Lena and Dirk, moved close enough to wrap a beefy arm around Brody's shoulder. "We'll be there at the hospital to meet you."

Tucker nodded, climbed into the van, and turned to

look out at Lori's family. They were wet and bedraggled, the hem of Lena's beautiful white dress trailing in the mud, Brody, Heck and Dirk sans jackets, with ties askew and shirts pulled half out of their trousers. Only Enid was crying, silent tears that tracked down haggard cheeks already wet with rain.

Then the med tech pulled the doors shut. The driver started the engine and off they went.

Tucker stayed out of the way as best he could in the cramped space. The E.M.T.s tended their patient, cleaning the wound, hooking her up to an IV drip, keeping close watch on her vital signs and communicating via radio with the hospital, so all would be ready for her when they arrived.

Watching them, so focused and efficient, Tucker found he felt a little bit calmer himself.

As soon as they had Lori settled, one of the E.M.T.s told him that the clubhouse, south of town and surrounded by a golf course, tennis courts, pool, formal grounds and beyond all that, acres of open land all around, was the only structure that had been hit. As far as they knew, Lori's was the sole injury—at least, so far.

In midride, the miracle Tucker didn't realize he'd been praying for happened.

Lori let out a low groan—and opened her eyes. Tucker, at the foot of the narrow portable cot where she lay, was right there waiting to give her a smile.

"Tucker?" She blinked and licked her lips and tried to lift the hand with the IV needle stuck in the back of it. She groaned again. "What…?"

"Easy, Mrs. Taylor…"

"It's all right, you're safe…" Making soothing noises, the E.M.T.s closed in.

Tucker craned to the side, so she could see him around the med techs bending close. "You were hit on the head—but you're going to be okay."

She asked, weakly, "Brody?"

"Safe," he told her. "He's with your folks. And as far as we know, everyone else is okay, too."

"Good," she whispered. "Good…"

Three hours later, near midnight, Tucker, Lena and Dirk sat in Memorial's main waiting room. Heck and Enid had taken Brody home. But Lena, still dressed in her limp wedding finery, said she was going nowhere until she was certain that Lori would be okay. Dirk kept close to his bride.

Tucker sat across from the newlyweds, his elbows braced on the chair arms, a paper cup of bad coffee balanced on his belly and his legs stretched out in front of him. He stared down at his scuffed dress shoes, not really seeing them.

Not seeing or thinking of anything, really.

Except Lori.

After she woke in the ambulance, she'd remained conscious: a good sign, the doctor had told them. In the hours since they arrived at the hospital, they'd done an MRI. It showed no evidence of a skull fracture, or of epidural or subdural hematoma: no blood on the brain, which could cause swelling and brain damage.

The wound had required twenty stitches, but the doctor said things were looking good. They would keep her at Memorial through the night for observation, just to be on the safe side. In the morning, barring complications, she would be released.

As Tucker sat there regarding his shoes, the hospital staff was in the process of moving her to a regular room. Once they had her settled, Tucker was planning to make sure they let him and Lena in to see her one more time, for a minute or two at least. If he got lucky, he might even be allowed to pull up a chair and stay the night. Tucker sipped the bitter hospital coffee, stared at his shoes some more, and hoped only for that: to be allowed to spend the night slouched in an uncomfortable chair in the room where Lori slept.

He was more certain than ever now. She was the woman for him. He marveled at himself. Until Lori, he realized, he'd never been all that certain of much of anything.

Fourteen days had gone by since his first real sight of her, at the Gas 'n Go. He'd held her in his arms only once—and still, he *knew.* Lori Lee Taylor was meant for him. And the very thought that he had almost lost her so soon after finding her...

Uh-uh. Not to be considered. It *couldn't* happen. He wouldn't let it.

And it *wasn't* happening, so he could stop worrying about it. The doctor had as good as promised them that she was going to pull through okay.

Across the short expanse of dark blue commercial carpet that covered the floor of the waiting area, in the chair next to Dirk's, Lena stretched and yawned. She leaned close to Dirk and whispered something in his ear.

Dirk grunted.

Lena, sliding a look at Tucker, nodded. "Oh, my yes. I know I'm right…"

Tucker sat up a little straighter and slugged back another gulp of bad coffee. "What?"

Lena braced her elbows on her knees and craned her head forward. She looked at him measuringly through those blue eyes so exactly like Lori's—but still, strangely, not like Lori's at all. "I think this is probably a dumb question. I mean, considering everything that's happened tonight. But, Tucker, I'm gonna ask it straight out, anyway. Are you in love with my sister?"

One thing about Lena. She never had a problem with cutting to the chase. Tucker opened his mouth to say, simply, *yes*—and then reconsidered. It seemed wrong, somehow, to go talking to Lena about how he felt. Lori was the one he ought to be talking to.

And he would. As soon as she was feeling better.

"Well, *are* you?" prodded Lena, when the seconds ticked by with no answer from him.

Dirk stirred in his chair. "Honey, leave the poor guy alone."

Lena smoothed her big, puffy skirt, sat up straight and spoke to her groom. "Well, she's my sister and I do want to know. Plus, if Lori married Tucker, I bet she'd move back to town…" She slid Tucker another glance. "I just want to say, you know, for the record, that I am all for that."

"Baby," said Dirk.

Lena gave him her sweetest smile. "What, darlin'?"

Dirk leaned across the space between the seats and

planted a quick kiss on his bride's pretty nose. "Some things are none of your damn business, that's what."

Lena heaved a windy sigh and flopped back in her chair. "Oh, well. I suppose you're right…"

The exchange surprised Tucker. The Lena he used to know would never have allowed any man to tell her a subject was none of her business. Apparently, true love really had changed her. Or maybe she'd just grown up a little.

Lena spoke again. "Well, Lori's going to be okay. I know it in my heart. And that makes me so happy—even if she does head back to San Antonio and I don't get to see her until the next time I go visit her." She plunked her elbows on her knees again and canted Tucker's way, bracing her pretty chin between her hands. "And, Tucker, you have saved her life and Brody's, too, and my family owes you. In a giant way. Forever and ever." Tucker didn't know quite what to say to that one—not that it mattered. Lena went on talking. "And even if it *is* none of my business, I did notice that you and my sister were together all afternoon. And having a mighty fine time, too. Weren't you? I'll bet you talked about just *everything*…"

Dirk warned, "Lena…"

She reached across and patted his arm. "It's all right, honey. I'm not gonna push." Then she told Tucker, "It's only that, well, after all you've done tonight, I want you to know that I truly do regret what Lori and I did to you, on prom night." Tucker frowned at her, not getting it. Her smooth brow crinkled. "Lori did tell you, didn't she?"

What they did *to him*.…

Must be the coffee. His stomach churned. He asked, with great care, "What did you do to me?"

"Oh." Lena blinked. "She didn't say?"

Dirk grunted some more. "Lena, what are you talking about?"

Lena looked from her groom to Tucker and back to Dirk again. "Oh, Lordy. I do believe I have gone and put my foot in it."

Dirk said, "Put your foot in *what?*"

Lena's cheeks flushed pink. She sat up straight and started waving her hands. "Oh, really. I mean, it's not that big a deal. After all, it was years and years ago and we were so young. And, um, pretty stupid, I guess. Pretty thoughtless. But, Tucker, you and I had broken up and I felt like I had to go to prom. I was up for prom queen and all. And folks always expected so dang much of me. So I did feel I should have put in an appearance— but at the same time, I didn't want to go. And Lori's date got sick on her. And she *did* want to go and…"

Tucker was getting it and it was not pretty. It was like some giant puzzle, random pieces flying everywhere, suddenly settling of its own accord into a recognizable whole. Tucker stared at Lori's sister in a kind of numb disbelief as it all fell together.

Lori in pink at the wedding, bringing that long-ago night to life all over again…

Her scent, so haunting and familiar…

The very feel of her in his arms…

The perfect, *remembered* fit of her mouth to his…

Lena was still chattering away. "And Tucker, look at it this way. Even if Lori hasn't told you yet about prom

night, well, what was the harm, really, in what we did?"
She fiddled with her big skirt, brushing at it, smoothing
it. "Oh, I am just making much too big a deal about
this." She flung her arms wide again. "It was a very
naughty little trick by two teenage girls, something you
have to know both Lori and I wish we had never so much
as considered...oh, and I do hope you'll forgive us—
both of us?"

Tucker couldn't have answered her if he'd wanted to.

Dirk said, "Lena. I'm lost here. Stop circling the
facts and spit 'em the heck out."

Lena let her flying hands fall to her lap. With another gusty sigh, she confessed to her husband, "Well, honey. Lori and I switched places on prom night eleven
years ago. I stayed home and pretended to be Lori. She
put on my pink prom dress and went to the dance with
Tucker, in my place."

"Well, I'll be damned." Dirk turned to Tucker. "And
you never knew?"

Somehow, Tucker managed to answer, "'Fraid not,"
in a calm voice that betrayed nothing of the emotional
tornado wreaking havoc within him. At the same time,
the last piece of the puzzle spun in his mind, stopped,
hovering in a holding pattern above the rest—and then
dropped neatly into place.

That final piece had Brody's face on it.

Chapter Nine

Maybe twenty seconds after Lena blew the whistle on that night eleven years ago, the doctor who'd taken charge of Lori when she reached the hospital appeared through the wide swinging doors to the patient area.

Lena, in a rustle of heavy skirts, jumped to her feet. "Dr. Zastrow, can we see her? Just for a minute or two, please?"

The handsome young doctor gave Lena a smitten-looking smile. "She's all settled. Resting comfortably— and as for paying her one more visit, how can I refuse such a beautiful bride?"

Dirk got up then, fast, and went to draw Lena close to his side, making it clear to the doctor that this particular bride was very much taken. "Thanks," he said flatly. "Which room is she in?"

Lena turned to Tucker, who'd yet to rise from his chair. "Tucker. Come on. We can go in now…"

He got up—not too fast; he felt slightly light-headed. And he took the few steps that brought him nose to nose with the good-looking surgeon. "You're sure. She's okay now?"

Zastrow smiled his movie-star smile. "She's doing very well. I think, by now, it's safe to say that she's out of the woods."

Lena quivered with impatience. "Tucker. Come on. Let's go…"

But Tucker wasn't going. He didn't want to see her right then. He *couldn't* see her—couldn't trust himself not to…

No. Better not.

He turned to Lena. "I think I should head on over to your folks' place, tell them the good news—and tell Brody, too, if he's still awake."

Brody, he thought, and then, impossibly, *my son…*

But wait. There was still that other guy from the night *after* the one she'd spent with him…

Or was there? Who the hell knew? Only Lori—sweet, beautiful Lori, who'd been lying to his face all along.

He still couldn't quite get his mind around the thousand and one ways she'd pulled the damn wool over his eyes. Lie after lie after lie. He had a lot to say to her and none of it was pretty—which meant he didn't dare to see her now. Not while she was flat on her back with twenty stitches in her head.

"But Tucker," Lena wheedled, "you don't need to go all the way over to the house. We can give my folks a call. And Lori's expecting you, looking forward to—"

"No." He fell back a step and put up a hand. "I should go. Tell her for me that I'll see her...real soon. Tell her to get well quick." Before Lena could argue any more, he spun on his heel and headed for the wide hallway that led out of there.

A minute or two later, he shoved through the hospital doors into the windy darkness of the night. The rain had stopped. Sometime during the long hours they'd waited to learn if Lori would make it, the wind had pushed the clouds along. Beyond the cover of the front entrance porte cochere, the sky was clear and thickly scattered with stars. He reached in his pocket for his keys...

And he remembered.

He had no damn car. It was somewhere in the club parking lot—maybe totaled and buried under the lifted-off roof of the clubhouse or an uprooted oak. Hell if he knew. And hell if he cared right at that moment.

He cared about getting where he was going, period—to the Billingsworth house, where he could see Brody. But Memorial was ten miles out of town and Tate's Junction was too small to support a cab company. Tucker stood there in the darkness, beneath the jut of the porte cochere, staring out at the stars, swearing under his breath and considering his options.

Dirk might loan him the keys to whatever vehicle he and Lena had taken to get to the hospital. But to get those keys he'd have to go back inside and find Lena's new husband, who was probably with her in Lori's room...

Uh-uh. Not happening.

Tucker got out his cell and actually raised a dial tone. But he flipped it shut before auto-dialing the ranch. He didn't want to drag anyone out of bed at that hour, not Tate and not Jesse Coutera, who ran the Double T garage. He could call a poker buddy, or his semiretired partner, Leland Hogan…

No. Same problem. It was a bad hour for asking favors. And he'd have to be civil to whoever he called; you didn't call a buddy at midnight asking for a ride and not make some kind of effort to explain why. Tucker wasn't feeling civil; he was in no mood to explain anything. He put his cell away.

Hands stuffed in his pockets, he started walking, thinking, as he strode across the parking lot, that walking was pretty stupid. It would take him hours to get to the Billingsworth place on foot.

But he didn't much care right then how long it took. He only knew he was going there, that when he arrived, he would see Brody and…

Hell. And what? He didn't know.

He didn't know anything, really. But then again, he'd been around the damn world and never really known where he was going. At least, tonight, his destination was clear.

The wind was in his face, warm and still smelling of rain. He peeled off his jacket, slung it over his shoulder and kept on walking.

Lena patted Lori's shoulder. "Dr. Zastrow says you're gonna be just fine. I am so relieved. I can't tell you. You gave us one whopper of a scare."

Lori stared at the empty doorway that Tucker should have come through. She lifted a careful hand and touched the bandage wrapped around the top of her throbbing head. Her head wasn't the only thing that hurt. Her whole body felt stiff and sore and she also had a kind of disembodied feeling, as if none of this was real.

And why hadn't Tucker come to see her again?

"I'll be back as soon as they'll let me," he'd whispered to her before he left her side the last time. He'd kissed her—a gentle brush of his lips against her own. "It won't be long," he promised.

So where was he now? She touched her mouth, where the feel of that feather-light kiss still lingered. Oh, she just didn't get it. "Tucker said he was going to Mama and Daddy's?"

Lena pasted on a bright smile. "That's right. He said he'd see you real soon and for you to get well." She patted Lori's shoulder some more.

Lori shut her eyes. When she opened them again, Lena was still there, looking down at her, smiling fondly.

What a sister, Lori thought. Lena's hair straggled free of her formerly elegant upswept do. She had a smudge of dirt on her cheek and her wedding dress was torn at the sleeve and stained with soot and mud—and still, she was forcing brave smiles.

I'm so very fortunate, Lori thought, to have a sister like this one: a sister who called all the time, whether I called her back or not. A sister who never gave up on keeping the family connection, a sister who didn't even hesitate to spend her wedding night at the hospital in her ruined bride's gown, waiting for a chance to pat me on the shoulder and tell me I'm going to be fine.

Lori said, softly, "Did I tell you? You're the most beautiful bride I ever did see."

Lena's eyes got misty. She sniffed. "Yes, I did look pretty amazing and gorgeous, didn't I?"

"You still do. Absolutely beautiful…"

Lena sniffed some more and lightly punched the shoulder she'd been patting. "Oh, stop."

"I'm grateful to have a sister like you."

"Now, I mean it. You will have me bawling my eyes out and we don't need that."

"I haven't always appreciated you and I know that."

"Okay, okay. You're definitely on to something, here. I won't deny it."

"But things are going to change, I promise. From now on, I'm going to work as hard as *you* always have, to keep that special connection between us."

"Good." Lena sniffed once more. And then she grinned. "Move home."

"I don't know about that—yet."

"Wow. You should get hit on the head more often—" Lena caught herself. "No. Scratch that." She pressed her hands together and cast her gaze heavenward. "I never meant that, Lord." She let her hands drop and looked ruefully at Lori. "I can't believe I said that. It was horrible, all of it, and I would never want anything like it to happen again."

Lori reminded her, "Still. You know what they say— bad luck at your wedding, good luck for the rest of your married life."

Lena sent a soft look over her shoulder at Dirk, who'd made himself comfortable in the corner chair. "I guess we're headed for the luckiest marriage in history."

"No doubt about it." Lori glanced toward the door again and sighed.

"What?" Lena prompted tenderly.

"I just wish Tucker had come on in here instead of heading for Mama and Daddy's."

"Oh. Well…" Lena was biting her lower lip.

Even with her body aching all over and her head pounding, Lori was getting the picture that something wasn't right. "Lena?"

"Um?"

"I think you'd better tell me what's going on."

An old farmer in an ancient pickup stopped for Tucker about a mile along the highway.

"You hear about that twister?" the farmer asked him as they rumbled down the road. "Blew away the dang country club." The farmer shook his grizzled head under his grimy Longhorn cap. "In the middle of a big weddin' party, too. D'ja hear 'bout that?"

Tucker made a noncommittal noise low in his throat and focused straight ahead.

"I heard everyone got out alive, though," said the farmer. "Praise the good Lord."

"Amen." Tucker never took his eyes off the dark highway in front of them.

The farmer said, "Son. You kinda look like you know exactly what I'm talking about. I'm guessing you're one of the ones who crawled out from under the ruins of that country club."

Tucker grunted and glanced down at his wrinkled, blood-spattered slacks and shirt. *Lori's blood,* he thought—and then put the thought away, shutting his mind against her. He gave the farmer a nod without glancing his way. "Yeah. I was there."

After a second or two, the old man asked, "You okay?"

Tucker looked over at him then. "No. But I'm working on it."

"Want to talk about it?"

"Sorry. Guess not."

"Good enough, then. Sit back and let me take you where you're goin'."

Ten minutes later, the farmer let him off in front of the handsome brick house where Lori had grown up. Tucker thanked the old guy and then stood there at the curb, staring vacantly after him as the rattletrap pickup rumbled away.

Once the taillights disappeared around the corner, Tucker blinked, shook his head, and turned to trudge up the front walk.

Dirk rose from the chair in the corner. "Lena, sweetheart." He wore the kind of look men wear when they know they're in the way. "I'll be in the waiting room." Lena went over and gave him a quick kiss.

Lori thanked him. "Dirk, you're about the best brother-in-law I ever had."

"Not to mention the only one." Chuckling, he left them.

Lena returned to Lori's bedside. "You know, maybe we ought to talk about this later." Careful of Lori's bandages, she reached out a hand and touched Lori's cheek. "You look real tired and I don't think it's a good idea for you to—"

Gently but firmly, Lori pushed her sister's hand away. "Something happened with Tucker. I know it. What?"

"Oh, well, I—"

"Lena. Just tell me. Please."

"Well, I'm not really sure. I mean, I could be wrong…"

"But…?"

Lena blew out a hard breath. "Okay. I think it kind of bothered him when I, um, let it drop about how you and me switched places on him on prom night."

Lori's heart stopped beating—and then lurched to racing life again. "You told him about prom night."

"Oh, Lori…"

Her mouth chose that moment to go desert-dry. She swallowed, then barely managed to croak, "Did you?"

"I, um…"

"Just answer me."

"Yes." Lena scrunched up her face as if she'd sucked a lemon. "It just kind of slipped out. I figured *you'd* already told him and I wanted him to know how bad I felt about us tricking him like that. By the time I realized you hadn't told him yet, I'd already said a big mouthful too much."

Lori swallowed, coughed. "Water…" Lena grabbed the foam cup from the retracting tray and handed it over. Lori sipped. Her throat soothed—if nothing else—she made herself ask, "So. He took it badly?"

"Oh, I don't know. He seemed okay—and come on,

it's not like it's some big, huge deal or anything. It was stupid and it was wrong. But it was also a long time ago and he and I had already decided it was over between us. And, well, I mean, it's the kind of thing we should be able to laugh about now. Don't you think?"

Lori let that question pass. "And after you told him?"

"He just got real quiet. Real strange, you know? And then, when the doctor said we could see you, he wouldn't come in with us." She paused to swipe a drooping auburn curl out of her eyes. "He just...didn't seem right."

"I see..." Boy, did she. She saw it all. And it wasn't good.

Her sister let out a frustrated cry. "I don't get it. Yeah, it was a mean trick to play on him, but it's not like it ruined his life or anything."

Lori stared at her sister. She thought of all the chances she'd had to tell him. She'd blown them all. And now it was too late. He already knew—and from what Lena had just told her, he hadn't taken the news well.

Lena let out a tiny sob. A tear slipped down her cheek, leaving a gleaming trail. "Oh, I'm so sorry. It looks like I've gone and messed everything up. I swear, I don't know why I have such a problem keeping my big mouth shut..."

Lori couldn't let her go on blaming herself. "You haven't messed anything up. *I* have."

Lena grabbed a tissue from the box on the tray. "Huh?" She honked into the tissue. "Come on. I was the one who had the idea for us to switch on prom night.

And I'm the one who blew it and told Tucker before you had a chance to tell him yourself. So it *is* my ”

Lori reached out and gently brushed her sister's arm. "Just believe me. It's not your fault."

"I don't see how you can say that."

"I know you don't. But you will."

Lena frowned. "Great. What you're tellin' me is that you're not going to explain to me what the heck is going on, right?"

"I can't. Not right now. I have to talk to Tucker first. But as soon as I do, I'll tell you everything, I promise."

"I just don't understand."

"You will. Right now, though, the main thing you need to know is that you didn't do anything wrong. What's wrong here is all *my* doing."

"But I don't…" Lena stopped in midsentence. Lori watched her sister's face and saw the exact moment when Lena caught on. "Or maybe I do," Lena said softly. "Prom night. You and Tucker…"

Lori gulped and nodded, thinking, *So much for my chance to talk it over with Tucker first.*

"You two didn't really go out for breakfast, did you?"

No more lies, Lori silently vowed. *Never again will a lie pass my lips.* She didn't let her gaze waver. "No. We didn't."

"And that guy, the next night. The one we all thought was Brody's father…there *was* no guy, was there?" Lori shook her head. Lena said, softly, "Wow."

Lori said, "I really messed up."

And Lena nodded. "Well, yeah. You really did."

* * *

Tucker paused with his hand raised to ring the bell. He stared at that heavy oak front door and remembered how he'd pounded on it that afternoon eleven years ago.

Lena had opened it and sent him away. He'd left not knowing that it wasn't even Lena he'd come to see.

Low in-ground lanterns shone from the flower beds. The porch light, a brass and beveled-glass creation suspended from a chain, glowed above his head. But as far as he could see, there were no lights on inside. If he rang the bell, he'd be getting them out of their beds.

So be it. He punched the doorbell and heard the chimes echo in the shadows beyond the door.

Then he waited. It didn't take long. Heck, in a plaid robe, his feet stuck in a pair of run-down moccasins, pulled open the door. At the sight of Tucker, his big, jowly face went slack. "Lori? Is she—?"

Tucker rushed to reassure the older man. "She's fine. Resting comfortably, they said. Lena's with her. I came to…let you know. That she's doing well…" Damn, that sounded lame.

But why wouldn't it? It *was* lame. Heck had heard the news already from Dr. Zastrow, hours ago, before he and Enid and Brody left the hospital.

Enid, wearing a long pink robe, her hair smashed flat on one side, appeared at the head of the stairs. "Heck? Who is it?"

"It's Tucker." The big man turned in the doorway and spoke to his wife. "He's come to tell us that Lori's doing just fine."

"Tucker!" Enid hurried down the stairs. "Come in, come in. Heck, honey, where are your manners?"

They led him to the kitchen and Enid brewed a quick pot of coffee. She poured him a mugful and fussed over him, offering eggs and toast if he wanted them. He declined, with thanks.

He didn't know what he'd expected, exactly. Maybe at least a little suspicion—on Heck's part, anyway. There was no real reason for Tucker to be showing up at their house well after midnight, rousing them from bed to tell them what they already knew.

But Heck and Enid didn't seem to care in the least that he really didn't need to be there, that the news he had for them wasn't news at all. And when he asked to see Brody, Enid popped right up and pushed in her chair. "Oh, he'll be so pleased. He was asking about you, just before he went to bed."

Tucker heard himself muttering, "Uh. He was?"

"Well, of course. You made quite an impression on him."

"I did?"

Heck chuckled. "Bound to impress a boy, when you save his life—and his mother's, too."

Enid added, looking misty-eyed, "Impresses a boy's grandparents, as well."

Heck said, "Damn, man. Believe it. You're almost as popular with Brody right now as that ugly mutt of yours."

Enid's misty smile widened. "You come on, now. This way…"

Tucker set down his coffee mug and fell in step behind her. She led him out of the kitchen, into the central hall and up the stairs, where she stopped at the first door on the right. She tapped lightly. They waited. No sound came from inside.

Enid put her finger to her lips, grasped the door handle and slowly pushed the door inward.

Light from the hallway poured into the room, a wedge of brightness across the single bed opposite where they stood. Brody was sound asleep, sprawled on his back, the covers kicked away.

He wore blue short-sleeved Bart Simpson pajamas. That persistent cowlick Tucker had noticed the afternoon before stuck up against the pillow—the cowlick so much like the one Tucker himself had always fought to tame. The light accentuated the shadow that defined the cleft in his chin—the cleft like the one Tucker saw every morning when he looked in the mirror to shave.

And not only the cowlick and the cleft chin. There was also the shape of his face and the curve of his mouth when he smiled.

Mine, Tucker thought.

There was no doubt about it. He should have seen it before. It really was damned amazing, how the truth had been right there in front of him for two weeks now, and he'd never seen it. He'd seen only what he *expected* to see.

Like Lena, that long-ago night...

He'd *expected* to see Lena that night. Lena, a vision in pink, whirling in his arms. Lena, nervous and so sweet, so achingly eager, naked beneath him, her soft lips forming his name.

Even that night, his senses had rebelled. He'd noticed—how different she seemed; her eyes softer, and her voice, too. Gentler, quieter; in a strange way, more feminine. That night, she wasn't the Lena he knew.

Because she wasn't Lena at all.

Silently, Enid pulled the door shut. She whispered, "Sorry. I hate to wake him…"

"It's all right," said Tucker. He'd seen what he needed to see.

Chapter Ten

The story of the twister that brought down the clubhouse on top of three hundred wedding guests made the first page of the *Abilene News-Reporter*. It also made the *Dallas Morning News*, though not the front page. Some eager newshound had gotten a great shot of the collapsed clubhouse under a lowering sky, with a bedraggled little knot of drenched wedding guests surveying the ruin. The picture was picked up by the wire services and popped up in papers all over the country. The story—a sound-bite-size version of it—even made it onto CNN and MSNBC.

Sunday afternoon, Dr. Zastrow released Lori into the loving care of her parents. Once she'd hugged her son and let her mother fuss over her for a while, Lori retreated to her room and called the Double T.

Miranda answered and asked her to please wait a moment.

Lori said, "Sure," and knew, beyond the last fading shadow of a very scary doubt, that Tucker would refuse to talk to her.

Then he picked up the phone. "Lori. Hello." And she didn't know which was worse: if he'd refused to talk to her at all, or his voice as it sounded now. Distant. Cool. Dangerously polite. "How are you feeling?"

"Better. Better all the time."

"That's good to hear."

"Tucker I…um…" Oh, God. How to even begin?

"Yeah, Lori?"

"Well, you know," she said, her voice wobbly and weak. "We really have to talk."

"Talk," he replied, as if mulling over the meaning of the word. "Yeah. I guess we do."

"I'm home—I mean, at my parents' house. I was thinking maybe you could come over and—"

He finished for her, "Have it out? Now?"

Have it out? Dread curled through her, burning a guilty path. "Well, yes. We could—"

"No," he cut her off again. "Not now. We'd better wait."

She put her hand against her bandaged head. Suddenly, it was aching like a sonofagun again. She dared to ask, "Wait for what?"

"How's your head? I'll bet it's still hurting pretty bad."

It seemed like a dangerous question, somehow. She started to lie and say no, it was fine. But then she reminded herself of how she would never lie again—not even a *little* one. "Yes. It still hurts."

"I thought so. We'd better wait a while."

"Until?"

"Until you're feeling better—in fact, I'm thinking you're going to want to cancel that appointment we had for tomorrow. You remember that appointment, Lori?"

"Of course I do."

"Speak up. I can't hear you."

"Yes," she said, out loud and clear. "I remember that we had an appointment tomorrow."

"An appointment to discuss the little matter you've known for, oh, eleven years or so that you really should talk to me about. Right?" She pressed her lips together and swallowed convulsively. He prodded, pumping up the volume, "Right?"

"Right," she said tightly. "Yes. To talk about—"

"Wait. Not now. Later."

She echoed, miserably, "Later?"

"Yeah."

"When?"

"Oh, come on, Lori. You've waited such a long time to tell me. It's not going to be any skin off your nose to wait a few more days."

His words hit home. Squarely. She wanted to crawl in a deep, dark hole and stay there—but she forced herself to argue, "I know Lena already told you, about that night. And I think you have to see that we—"

"I want you feeling good. Strong. When I talk to you."

"Tucker. Please. I just—"

"Thursday. I'll call you Thursday. We'll see how you're doing then."

"But I—"

"And in the meantime, I'd like to see Brody. Would that be all right with you?"

"See Brody?" She didn't know why that surprised her. Of course, he'd want to see Brody.

"Is that a problem for you?" Beneath the fake-cordial tone, his deep voice vibrated with subtle threat.

"No. Not at all." God. They sounded like a couple getting a divorce and discussing visitation rights. A couple getting a divorce—though they'd never gotten near being married in the first place.

"All right, then," he said. "I'd like to pick him up at five in the afternoon tomorrow. I'll have him back to you by nine. Is that acceptable?"

"I…yes. That's fine." She had a thousand questions. She hardly knew how to start asking them—and he didn't seem especially eager to give her any answers. "What will you tell him?"

He made a sound, kind of like a laugh, but with absolutely no humor in it. "As of now, nothing. I want to take it slow, let him get to know me better before I go springing any big surprises on him."

"Oh. Well. That sounds, um, wise."

"Thank you," he said, as if he didn't mean it in the least. "So I'll call him—a little later, this evening. I'll ask him if he wants to come out to the ranch tomorrow, to ride Little Amos, swim, cook hot dogs, play with Fargo…" His voice trailed off.

She thought, sadness squeezing her throat, of that night a little over a week ago, that lovely night when she and Brody had gone to visit him, together.

That night seemed like eons ago now.

"Lori. You with me?"

With him? Not in the least. "I'm here. It's all fine. Just fine."

"All right, then. If he says yes to coming on out here tomorrow—" he would, and they both knew it "—I'll have him ask you. You will agree."

Irritation made her head throb harder. "I already said it was okay with me."

"Good. And if he wants you to come, too, you'll say you don't feel up to it."

She *didn't* feel up to it. So that wouldn't be a lie. She leaned back on the bed and shut her eyes. "Yes. All right."

"If it goes well, tomorrow, I'll ask him to come Wednesday evening, too. You'll tell him that you don't feel up to going Wednesday, either."

She asked, though she knew she shouldn't, "What if I *do* feel up to it Wednesday? What should I say then?"

"You'll think of something, I'm sure."

"I'm not going to lie to him."

He did laugh, then, she was sure of it. A very mean laugh. "That's a good one. Coming from you." She opened her mouth to call him hardhearted—and then shut it. The remark *had* been cruel. But it was also the truth. She'd told a boatload of lies and it would only be lying some more to pretend that she hadn't.

He said, "Any more objections?"

She lifted her hand and rested it, very carefully, on the bandage that covered her pounding forehead. "You sound like a lawyer."

"That's because I am one. I'll talk to you Thursday."

"Wait. I…" But it was too late.

He'd already hung up.

Monday, Lena and Dirk were set to leave on the two-week honeymoon they'd postponed until Lena could be certain that her twin would recover. Lori was still upstairs in bed, with the curtains drawn, when Lena dropped in to tell the family goodbye.

"Mornin'." Lena poked her head in the bedroom door. "Wake up, Sleeping Beauty. It's ten o'clock and it's too dark in here." Lena bounced into the room and flung the curtains wide. Lori groaned at the brightness of the harsh morning light. "There, now, isn't that better?"

"Not particularly." Lori scooted to a sitting position, squinting her good eye as it adjusted to the brightness. Since the other eye was swollen shut, the morning glare didn't bother it at all.

Lena dropped to the bed. "How you feelin', hon?"

"Not so great."

"We're off to the airport in an hour. And you've got a real shiner there. All purple and swollen up. Not too attractive."

"Gee. Thanks."

"Get over here." Lena held out her arms.

Lori went into them. "You have a terrific time, okay?" She gave her sister a good, hard hug.

"Oh, I will. Bahama-mama, that's me. I can't wait till Dirk sees this itty-bitty thong bathin' suit I have bought. Oh, my, and the lingerie…I got a trunk full, been buying it for months now. Me and my darlin' and Victoria's

Secret are going to have ourselves one fine ol' time."
Lena took her by the shoulders and held her away.

Lori pulled back, met her twin's bright eyes and
thought how much she loved her. "You know…"

"Say it."

"All these years, I thought you'd be so mad at me,
when you found out."

Lena shrugged. "Well, I probably would have been.
Way back when. But now? Honey, it was so long ago.
I look back and I don't feel a thing—well, except sympathy pains. It must have been so terrible for you, on
your own and pregnant, keepin' that secret, having to tell
all those lies…"

Lori sat up straighter. "I didn't have to tell them. I
chose to."

"Well, you *were* seventeen and—"

Lori put up a hand. "Don't make excuses for me. I've
made too many for myself."

The sisters shared a long look of perfect understanding, then Lena asked, "So what the heck's going on
with Tucker, anyway? Mama said he didn't come by all
day yesterday."

Lori stiffened. "What did you tell her?"

"Relax. Not a dang thing. For once, I am keeping out
of it. I told Mama if she wants to know about you and
Tucker, she'd better ask you."

"You're the best."

"I certainly am."

Lori slumped back among the pillows. "As far as
Tucker and me, I don't know…"

"You should call him today."

"I already did, yesterday. I tried to tell him I just want to talk about everything now, to get it over with. He wouldn't listen. He says he wants me feeling good—when he lays into me."

"Maybe that's smart—that you wait till you're feeling a little better, I mean."

"Oh, Lori. This is bad. I mean, really bad. He's so mad and he won't talk to me. It's awful."

Lena gave her a chiding look. "Well, hon, you have to admit he's got a right to be mad."

"I know he does."

"You just be patient, now. You'll work it out."

"I don't know. I just don't know…"

Lori stewed all day about whether or not she should be downstairs to greet Tucker when he showed up to get Brody. In the end, she decided against it. She looked truly terrible—her forehead, on the left side, beneath the bandage, was all black and blue, her left eye big and purple as a ripe plum. She just didn't want him to see her that way. She knew he'd feel sorry for her.

She could do without his pity, thank you very much.

He showed up at five on the dot and whisked their son off in the back seat of a big black Cadillac. She stood in her bedroom window and watched the car drive away.

Four hours later, she was waiting in the same spot, watching for their return, with the window open a crack. At two minutes after nine, the big car slid up to the curb and Brody jumped out before the chauffeur could get around and open the door for him.

"It's all right, Jesse," she heard Brody say to the

driver. "I like to open doors for myself." The driver went back around the front of the car as Brody leaned in the still-open rear door. "Bye, Tucker. See you Wednesday…"

So, then. Wednesday was a go.

She knew it was a good thing, for her son to finally get to know his natural father. She was glad for that.

She honestly was.

Everything else, though?

What an awful, ugly mess.

Tuesday, Enid took her to see Doctor Zastrow. The doctor removed her bandages, prodded the healing gash at her temple and told her things were looking good. As he bandaged her back up—a much smaller bandage than before—she joked that he must be blind, considering that the top half of her face on the left side bore a startling resemblance to an eggplant.

He told her what she already knew: the swelling would go down, the stitches would be absorbed, the scar would heal and the bruises would fade. "Give it time. And if in six months you're not happy with that scar, a little minor plastic surgery will have you looking as beautiful as ever." She realized he was right on the verge of flirting with her.

She broke eye contact. And not because he seemed like the kind of man who flirted as a matter of course—though he definitely did. No. She looked away because of Tucker. If she was going to do any flirting, she wanted it to be with him. Which, considering the way things stood between them, was right next-door to pitiful.

On the way back to the house, Enid daintily tried to find out what had happened between her daughter and Tucker.

"Lori, hon, your father and I have been wondering—"

Lori cut her off at the pass. "Is this about Tucker, Mama?"

Enid nervously clenched and unclenched her slim hands on the steering wheel. "Well, sweetie, he did save your life and he seemed so attentive and then—"

"Not now, Mom. I can't talk about it now."

Enid didn't press her further. Lori was grateful for that.

Wednesday, she decided she was through hiding in her room. When Tucker arrived for Brody, she answered the door herself.

His face, all ready with a smile of greeting, went blank at the sight of her. "Lori."

"Hello, Tucker."

"That eye looks pretty bad."

She drew herself up. "It's better than it was. In fact, I'm feeling pretty good. By tomorrow, I'll be ready for that long talk we need to have."

"We'll see—Brody here?"

"You know he is." She stepped back so he could enter as Brody pounded down the stairs.

"Hey, Tucker!"

The look on Tucker's face at the sight of his son made her heart squeeze up tight in her chest. "Hey, bud. There you are. Let's get the heck out of here." He turned and headed down the front steps.

"Okay!" Brody flew by her, close on Tucker's heels.

Halfway down the walk, he paused to look back at her. "Mom? You could go with us, if you want…"

Tucker stopped in midstride and turned to face her again, his eyes flat, giving her nothing.

She beamed a thousand-watt smile at her son. "Uh. No. I'll stay home tonight. You have a great time."

Brody ran back and hugged her. "Love you, Mom…"

She was careful, not to hold him too tight. "Love you, too…"

His arms dropped away and he was off again, racing down the steps and along the walk, yanking open the rear door of the big black car and sliding inside.

Lori stepped back into the house and quickly shut the door. She was simply unable, at that moment, to watch the gleaming Cadillac drive away from her carrying her child.

She turned from the shut door to see her parents standing together near the foot of the stairs wearing twin expressions of sad bewilderment.

In their loving, confused faces she saw her secret reflected. She saw what the secret had done to her family, how it had ripped right through the fabric of it, tearing a ragged hole of hurt and misunderstanding every bit as wide as the one that yawned now between her and the father of her child.

Her dad and mom—and Lena—they were her people. And she had deserted them, left them behind. She'd made a new life for herself without them in it.

Because she was a coward unwilling to face the consequences of the huge mistakes that she had made.

No more, she thought, the words as loud and final

as gunshots inside her head. *No more secrets and no more lies.*

She lifted her head high. "Mama, make a fresh pot of coffee. You and me and Daddy have to have a little talk."

Chapter Eleven

The kitchen was way too quiet when Lori finished revealing the truth behind all the lies.

Finally, her mother said, "Oh, hon. What a terrible mess. I am so, so sorry…"

Her dad hung his big head. "Lori—girl, I've always wanted to tell you, but I never knew how…"

Lori couldn't get over how light she felt, suddenly. Unshackled. Released at last from the dragging weight of the secret and all the lies and evasions that had followed after.

"Tell me now, Daddy," she said. "Because I promise, I'm listening."

He raised his head and looked at her through haunted eyes. Her heart went out to him. For the first time she understood how much he had suffered for his part in what had happened eleven years before.

Heck said, "I always used to worry…back when you and your sister were growing up. I worried about Lena. All the boys were after her. I was sure she was headed for trouble. But you? I never lost a wink of sleep over you. You were always so smart and quiet, with no time or inclination to tease and flirt and string the boys along. And you had straight-As and all those colleges were after you, throwin' scholarships at you…" Heck folded both arms on the table and paused to look down at the big Rolex watch he always wore with such pride. He seemed to study that watch, as if the face of it could tell him more than the time.

Enid reached over and brushed his shoulder—a light and tender touch of wifely reassurance. "Go on, honey. Tell her. She wants to hear it."

Heck looked up again and met Lori's eyes. "I guess I kind of went crazy, when you turned up in the family way. I didn't know how to handle it. I was not prepared. I wanted so much for you—expected so dang much of you—more, I see now, than I ever expected of your sister. I was hopping mad and I scared you to death, with all my shouting, my hard threats and carrying on." He repeated, "I scared you to death. And then I sent you away. I sent you away—" His voice broke. He looked down again and that time, it was obvious he wasn't looking at his watch. His thick shoulders shook. "And you never came back. I am sorry. I never should have sent you away."

Lori reached across the table and clasped her father's

beefy arm. "Daddy," she said. "I forgive you. And, I did come back. I'm here now, aren't I?"

He lifted his head then. Tears tracked down his ruddy sun-creased cheeks. He swiped them away with the back of his hand and blustered, "Will you look at me? Bawlin' like a damn baby. Don't know what the hell's gotten into me."

"I'm here, Daddy," Lori softly said, once more. "I really am."

Her father looked straight at her, then. He was smiling through his tears.

Later, around the dinner table, Enid asked about Tucker.

Lori confessed, "I don't know any more than you do. From his actions, I'd say it's pretty clear he intends to be a real father to Brody."

"Brody hasn't said a word, so I'm guessing he doesn't know yet...that Tucker's his dad?"

Lori shook her head. "Tucker wants Brody to have a chance to get to know him first. He wants to break it to him gently. I'm going to try to respect Tucker's wishes on that. So unless Brody asks you directly, please keep what I said tonight to yourselves for a while."

Enid said, "Whatever you need from us—but if he does ask?"

"Then tell him to come and talk to me. I don't want Brody lied to."

Her father nodded. "We understand."

Enid said, "And what about *you* and Tucker? It did seem, until just lately, that you two were...becoming close."

"Mama, I just don't know. Right now, between Tucker and me, it doesn't look too good."

Thursday afternoon at four-thirty, Tucker sat behind the desk in his study at the Double T, a whiskey on ice in a crystal glass at his elbow and Lori on his mind. He reached for the phone—and it rang.

Impatient to get rid of whoever it was and get on to the phone call to Lori, he pushed the talk button and put it to his ear without checking the display. "Tucker Bravo. What?"

"It's Lori."

He wrapped his hand around his drink—and then let go of it. "Beat me to the punch, huh?" It came out sounding lazy and a little bit mean. Just how he felt right then—at least the mean part.

He heard her suck in a breath. Then she rattled off, as if she'd been rehearsing it, "Tucker, I'm fine now. I'm well enough to talk. And we do have to talk. We have to come to some sort of reasonable arrangement about Brody and the future and what we intend to—"

He didn't need to hear it. "Lori."

There was a silence down the line. And then, tightly, she asked, "What?"

"Come out here, to the ranch."

"Now?"

"Yeah. Now. Come to the front door of my wing, the South Wing."

"I—"

"Yes or no?"

Another silence, then, "Yes. Twenty minutes." He

heard the click. Score two for her: *she'd* called *him*. And she'd hung up before he could hang up on her.

The blood pumped hard and fast through his veins. He felt ready for battle. Impatient and exhilarated.

Probably a bad sign.

A woman Lori didn't recognize answered her knock. The woman led her through the high-ceilinged foyer and into the beautiful, spare-looking South Wing living room, an airy space done in golds and browns, accented with black. That other time, two weeks ago, the room had seemed so relaxing and welcoming.

Not now.

Tucker sat on a coffee-brown sofa. He didn't get up. "Thank you, Mrs. Haldana," he said to the stocky, gray-haired woman. He picked up the full glass from the side table at his elbow. It had a watered-down look about it, as if he'd poured it a while ago and then decided not to drink it. "Want something—whiskey? Water? Both?"

"No, thank you."

"All right, then." He set the drink down without bringing it to his lips and turned to Mrs. Haldana. "I won't need you anymore tonight." The woman nodded and left them. He turned his shuttered gaze on Lori again. "Sit down," he said.

She almost refused, but then realized he would probably take it as an offensive move. She really, truly did not want to fight with him. So she perched across the glass coffee table from him, on a sofa identical to the one where he sat.

He said, "That eye still looks pretty bad. How are things under the bandage?"

She shrugged. "It burns and itches, alternately, which means it's healing, so I'm not complaining. I'm feeling better every day. And that's not what I came here to talk to you about. I…" She drew a complete blank. There was so much to say, she hardly knew where to begin.

He didn't help her out. He just sat there. Watching. Waiting.

She forged ahead again. "I know, I truly do, that there's nothing I can say that will excuse my not telling you that you have a son. I was wrong, and I know it. I knew it all along. I…well, I did try, to get a hold of you. When Brody was a baby, I found out where you lived in Austin. I went down there. You were gone by then, though, and the guy who answered the door didn't know where you went. I wrote letters. More than one. But you went off to Europe and I didn't know where to send them. I tried the Austin address, hoping it might be forwarded. It came back. So I sent one here, to the Double T, thinking your grandfather would send it on to you. I guess he did. But that letter never reached you, either. It came back to me with French postal marks all over it, unopened, and I—"

His low growl of fury shut her up. He demanded, "What about just gutting it up and getting your butt out here, to the ranch? What about telling my granddaddy that you'd had my baby? Did you try that?"

"No. I—"

"'No' about says it all. You didn't come here and talk to my grandfather—though we both know damn well what Ol' Tuck was like. If he'd known he had a grandson, Granddaddy would have tracked me down. He'd have gone to the ends of the earth to get me back home and married to the mother of my child."

Lori knew he was right. She had no excuses, yet somehow she couldn't stop herself from trying to make him see how it had been for her. "Oh, Tucker, I was so young. And I felt so alone. I was scared of Ol' Tuck. Everybody was. You know that. And really, I didn't even *know* you. That night, the night of the prom, I—"

"Yeah. That night." He sat so still, a frightening stillness, one that radiated cold rage. "Now you mention it, there was that, too, wasn't there? That night you took your sister's place. That night you let me call you Lena, over and over and over again. That night you smiled and sighed and went with me to that motel room. That night you let me take your clothes off you and touch your naked body and lay you down and call you Lena some more, while I was buried inside you. What about that night?"

She had nothing to say. There *was* nothing to say. "I was wrong. I know it. I should have—"

"Do you think I give a good damn about what you should have done? I'm not there yet. I'm still back with what you did. I'm back with calling you Lena while I was loving you, I'm back to that second time, when I'd used my one condom, when I was so gone on you, I had some crazy idea it didn't matter, if we made a baby. It didn't matter because I was staying right here, in town, because we'd be getting married anyway. Oh, yeah. I'm still back with what you did. Still back with the day *af-*

ter that night, when I came to your door and you let Lena answer it and send me away."

"It was…I wasn't thinking straight. I got home and I looked at Lena and I felt so low, so bad, like I'd done something so awful, behind her back."

"Because you had."

She pulled her shoulders back. "Yeah. Yeah, I know it."

"And the next night—that guy everyone thinks you met. What about him?"

She said, in a whisper, through her clutching throat, "There was no guy."

He grunted again. A sound of purest disgust. "No guy."

She coughed to make her throat open up. "That's right. Only you. I…well, I always wanted you, when we were kids. I would see you in town and at school and I would hope and pray that you would notice me. But you didn't. It was Lena you noticed, Lena who got to be your girl. I accepted that—or I thought I had. And then Lena broke up with you and she didn't want to go to prom with you and—"

He waved a hand. "Back to that other guy. The one who didn't exist."

She made herself nod. "Okay. What about him?"

"You didn't hesitate, did you, to let people think what was easiest for you? The whole damn town jumped to conclusions about how you ended up pregnant—and you let them. You let everyone think some stranger was Brody's father."

"Oh, Tucker, my dad was yelling all the time, making threats. He said he was going to find out who got me pregnant and—"

"I don't want to hear it. I have more questions."

Her mouth tasted of sawdust. The long gash at her temple felt like someone was sticking needles in it.

Too bad, she thought.

She knew it was only right, that she sit there. That she take whatever he felt he had to dish out. It wasn't much, wasn't anywhere near enough, but it was the very least she could do.

And it was a first step. She had to believe that. For him to be so angry, he had to *care.* If he didn't care, he wouldn't be facing her down now. If he didn't care, he would have just informed her of what he planned to do about Brody and left it at that.

"Your husband," he said. "What lies did you tell him about my son?"

"I didn't tell my husband lies. Henry knew the truth. I told him everything, before we were married."

"And what? He told you not to worry, that it was just fine with him that Brody's father had no idea he existed?"

She stopped him on that one. "No. Brody *does* know, that he had a…a natural father, that Henry was his stepdad."

He looked at her through narrowed eyes. "And just what does Brody think happened to his *natural* father?"

"I told him it didn't work out, between his father and me. That his father went away before he knew that he had made Brody. That someday, when the time was right, we'd find his dad somehow."

"When did you tell him all this?"

"Years ago. He was three. It was right before I married Henry."

"And since then?"

"He doesn't ask. Oh, Tucker. You have to see. He's had a…happy life. He loved Henry and he accepted him, as his dad. I always knew that someday he'd have questions, that someday he'd need to know you."

"Someday…"

"You have to understand…"

"But I don't, Lori. I don't get it. I don't get any of it. You're telling me that your husband knowingly stole my son from me."

"He didn't. He never could. It's only…well, Henry was sterile. And he'd always wanted children. He said that you were long gone and he thought it was for the best if we just let things go along the way that they were. I'm ashamed to say it, but, by then, that was just what I wanted to hear. We got married. Henry treated Brody like a son. We were…happy, the three of us."

"Happy." He made it sound like a dirty word.

"Yes."

"And you gave up all attempts to get a hold of me?"

"Yes. That's right. It was all wrong, what we did, Henry and me. And he knew it in his heart. It was his last wish, before he died, that I track you down and tell you the truth."

"So what you're saying is that whenever you finally did get around to telling me—if you ever did—it would have been for your dead husband's sake."

"I didn't say that. I *never* said that."

"And your husband's been dead, what? Over a year? And I've been right here, in the Junction, just about the whole damn time."

She refused to let her gaze shift away. She looked him straight in the eye. "I don't expect you to under-stand. I loved my husband. He had come into my life at a time when I was barely holding on, feeling…so bad about myself, about what a mess I'd made of my life. I was disconnected from my family, working overtime to take care of me and Brody, trying to be a good mother to him. Henry…showed me how to live. Really, I grew up, took charge of my own life, while I was married to Henry. I wasn't much good for a while there after I lost him. I couldn't…deal with anything beyond getting by, day to day. I knew—even before Henry died—that I would tell you. But after I lost him, I needed time to face up to the job."

"More excuses. More lies." A cold smile curved the corners of Tucker's mouth. "It's time to get straight about this, Lori. You were never going to tell me. Not really. Were you?"

Outrage had her heart slamming against her breast-bone. She quelled that outrage, ordered her damn heart to slow down. From the way she'd behaved, what else was he to think, but that she would have always found some reason to keep the truth from him?

She spoke flatly. "I was going to tell you Monday. I made that appointment to do it. I would have done it then."

"I don't believe you."

She pressed her lips together, holding in the hot de-nials that rose to her lips. What good would denials do? He didn't believe her and she had no right to imagine that he should.

He said, "Why Monday? Why did you think you had

to wait? Why not any one of those times you saw me after you got into town? Why not that night you came out here with Brody, that night we talked for hours about everything *but* the one thing that mattered most. Why not then?"

"It wouldn't have been right, not with Brody there. And I had planned from the first to wait until after the wedding. I wanted Lena to have her big day. If the story got out, I was afraid it might ruin things for her."

He shook his head. "Excuses," he said. "That's all you've got for me, isn't it?"

"No. That's not so. There *are* no excuses and I know there aren't. But you asked. So I answered you. I came here, back to town, for two reasons. My sister's wedding—and *you*. I planned to stay an extra week after the wedding was over. That week was so I'd have plenty of time to see you, to tell you what you had a right to know. I had it all worked out. Once the wedding was over, I'd get in touch with you, meet you someplace private and tell you that you had a son. I assumed I'd have zero contact with you until it was time to say what needed saying. How was I to know I'd run into you the minute I drove into town. How was I to know I'd *keep* running into you? How was I to know that I…" She faltered.

He prodded, "That you, what?"

Her cheeks burned with a sudden, hot blush. "Look. It doesn't matter."

He wouldn't let it be. "What? How were you to know *what*?"

"It doesn't—"

"What?"

She shut her eyes. It didn't help. When she opened them again, he was still there. Waiting, his square jaw set and his brown eyes hard as agates. She told him, very quietly, "How was I to know that I would find myself falling for you all over again? That one look at you and I'd feel like I felt back in high school, that I'd be mooning around, longing for a glance from you, a gentle word. A sweet, tender kiss."

She looked away, toward the tall windows that flanked a glass door and a deep back porch. It was beautiful out there, so green and lush. She wished she could leap up, fling open the door, race down the porch steps and run across that long slope of thick lawn—run and run and never stop. She faced him again, her heart squeezing tight inside her chest. It hurt—a thousand times worse than the needles poking into her brow—to look at him. So big and handsome, with his sexy full mouth, that sun-kissed brown hair and those gorgeous dark eyes—eyes that seemed to bore through her, a mouth set against her.

"I didn't like it," she said flatly. "I didn't like being so strongly attracted to you after all these years. That's the honest, unvarnished truth, whether you're able to believe me or not. I didn't expect it and it confused me, terribly, to find myself still wanting you after all this time. I thought I had grown out of you. But since I've been back in town, I'm a mixed-up teenager all over again. I've made the same bad choices I made back when. I messed things up royally, the same way I did when we were kids."

"So that's what I am to you. A bad choice?"

"That's not what I said. You're twisting my words."

"You amaze me. You are one piece of work. You're attracted to me. And that's why you kept my son from me all over again. And somehow, you've got the idea that your telling me this will get you off the hook now?"

"I didn't say I thought it would get me off the hook. I never said that." She had to actively resist the need to bring her hand to her forehead, to press the bandage that covered the now-throbbing gash.

"Good," he said, "Because you're not off the hook, Lori. Not for this. You never will be."

She folded her hands in her lap—good and tight—and looked down at them, hard. "Gotcha." She faced him. "So how about this? We tell Brody right away that you're his father. Then we can—"

"No."

Had she heard wrong? "Wait a minute. You *don't* want to tell him?"

"Not yet."

"But he—"

"You said it yourself. He thinks of that husband of yours as his father. He's mentioned him to me. More than once. It's 'my dad,' this and 'Dad used to' that. Whatever I think of the man who knowingly tried to steal my son from me, I'm not going to—"

It was too much. "Tucker. Stop. I understand that you're angry—beyond angry, even. And I know that you have every right to be. But Henry was a good father to Brody. A damn good father. You've said yourself what a great kid Brody is. A great kid doesn't happen in a vacuum."

"Exactly," he said.

And her mouth almost dropped open. "You...*agree* with me?"

"Yeah." *He agreed.* She could hardly believe it. It was a first, for this particular conversation. "Brody's a hell of a kid and that husband of yours did a bang-up job with him. I want to give Brody time to accept me in his life, to get used to the idea that I'm going to be around from now on."

In spite of all the hard things he'd said to her, at that moment, she felt so sad for him. He really didn't know his son at all.

And whose fault was that?

Hers. The fault was all hers.

"Tucker," she said carefully. "Give Brody a little credit. He's really so smart and...down to earth. He's already gotten to know you. He thinks you're terrific. You can tell him, now. He can take it."

"No." He gave her a look, dead-on and imperious. Never before had he reminded her of Ol' Tuck. But at that moment, he did. He said in a tone both flat and final, "It's too soon."

"You're wrong about that."

"Think what you want. It's my decision." He said it as if it didn't even occur to him that she might dare to go against him.

Ol' Tuck. Definitely. Way too much like Ol' Tuck.

And he was right. It *was* his decision. She wouldn't go against him, not about this. He had the right to tell Brody in his own way and his own time.

She suggested, with care, "How can I help you, to get to know your son?"

He nodded, a regal dip of his head. "Yeah. It's time we talked specifics."

Her heart was racing again. And her palms had gone clammy. She feared the worst. That he'd say he was suing her for custody, that he'd demand she turn Brody over to him.

If he did that, all that would be left for them was an ugly legal battle, with Brody at the center of it, suffering for her bad choices, her lies—and for his father's vindictiveness.

She tamped her fears down and tried to speak calmly. "Yes. All right. I, um, realize you're going to want to spend some time with him—on a regular basis. I think we can work together to—"

"When does his school year start?"

Where was he headed? And why did she have a sinking feeling it wasn't anywhere that she would want to go? "Late August," she said. "The twenty-fourth or twenty-fifth, I think."

He laid it on her. "I want you and Brody to move in here, with me, right away. I want a chance with him, a chance to catch up after all the years I didn't have with him. A couple of months of him living with me should go a long way toward that. Before he leaves to go back to school, I will have told him that I'm his father."

"But I don't—"

"I'm not finished." He gave her a long look. It wasn't a friendly one. Then he continued, "I need you here, at first, to ease the way. I want him to feel comfortable and I want the visit to seem…natural to him. It won't seem that way if you don't stay here, too."

She spoke up, though she knew he wouldn't like what she said. "You *could* just tell him who you are."

"I already told you. Not yet."

"Tucker, I don't like this. I think—"

"I don't care what you don't like, or what you think. I need you here, so my son will feel comfortable about staying with me. And I think you owe it to me—and to him—to be here, for a while, at least. Once Brody knows the truth, once he's had time to adjust to being with me full-time, you'll be free to go back to San Antonio. You can return to pick him up a few days before school starts."

"And...after that?"

"After that, I'll want time with him. Holidays, summers and school vacations, anyway. And we'll be going to court."

She felt vaguely ill. "Court?"

"He's my son. I want it legal. I want a document that says he's a Bravo attached to his birth certificate."

"Yes. All right. Of course."

He said, "The adoption might present complications."

"The adoption?" She didn't follow at first. Then the light dawned. "Oh. No. Henry never adopted Brody."

"Why not?"

"We decided against it. For the reasons you just gave. When it came down to it, Brody was—and is—your son."

"Plus, if I ever did find out you let another man have my son, who the hell knows what kind of trouble I might have made for your happy little family, right?"

She sucked in a long breath. "That's right."

There was more to it.

Henry had pushed—hard—for the adoption. He'd insisted it was the best thing, that Tucker never had to know. Lori had said no. In the end, she couldn't do that. Tucker was Brody's father and that could never be erased.

But there was no point in going into all that now. It would have served no real purpose, would have only sounded like more excuses, an attempt to make herself look a little less reprehensible—at the expense of her dead husband.

Tucker said, "You've been calling him Brody *Taylor,* though, haven't you? Even though his birth certificate gives him your maiden name?"

"Yes."

"No more. When he goes back to school, he's going as a Bravo."

"Yes. I'll see to it."

"You bet you will." He looked at her as if he wouldn't trust her to pass him the salt at the dinner table.

Her temper flared again. She doused it, suggesting carefully, "And for now, maybe we should just take it one day at a time. Just get through the summer and not worry about all the rest of it until we have to."

He sat forward. "You're saying you'll do it. You'll give me what I want. Tomorrow, you and Brody will move in here, with me."

"Yes."

His eyes darkened—with triumph and something more...

Something that brought a tiny, valiant flame of hope rising to flicker within her.

Was it possible?

Could he, just maybe, want more from her than her support while he got to know his son? Deep down, did he have some faint intention of trying to make it work between them, after all? Did he want her with him, at his house, at least a little bit for her own sake?

She wondered—and then she put that tiny hope away. It didn't matter. Not right then. Right then, her lies and her betrayals stood high as a fortress wall, thick and impossible to scale, between them. He didn't trust her—with valid reason. He had disconnected from her. And any dreams she might have finally admitted to having about the two of them…

Well, this didn't look like a situation where dreams were all that likely to come true.

What mattered now was that Tucker and Brody should have their time together; her job would be to do all she could to make that happen.

She said, "We'll move in tomorrow."

"All right, then," he agreed. "Let's get through the summer. We'll worry about the rest of it when fall comes around."

Chapter Twelve

That evening, after Brody was in bed, Lori sat her parents down at the kitchen table and told them that she and Brody would be staying at the Double T for a while.

"You don't seem all that happy about it," her father remarked with a frown.

"It's what Tucker wants, to have some time with his son."

"And what about you, Lori-girl? What do *you* want?"

"Right now, I just want to do my part to make sure they get the time together that they need."

Her mother asked, "And you and Tucker?"

Okay. Maybe she couldn't quite banish that thin flame of hope that she and the father of her son might find their way to each other, at last. But it was just that:

a hope. Nothing more. "Mom, there *is* no me and Tucker. Not now, anyway."

"But do you think that you could—?"

"Enid." Heck scooted his chair closer to his wife and threw an arm across her slim shoulders. "It's Lori's life. We gotta learn to step back and let her live it."

"I know. It's only—"

He pulled her closer and chucked her under the chin. "Let it be, now."

Enid wrinkled up her nose at him—and conceded, "Oh, all right."

Lori got up, went around the table and planted a kiss on her father's beard-rough cheek. "I love you, Daddy— Mama, you, too…"

Heck beamed up at her. "Now, that there's exactly what we like to hear."

Lori told Brody the plan the next morning at the breakfast table.

"All summer?" Brody frowned and scooped up another spoonful of Cheerios. They were alone in the Billingsworth kitchen. Heck had headed for his dealership and Enid was grocery shopping.

Lori set down her coffee cup and smiled her brightest smile. "Until the end of August. Two whole months, almost, at the Double T. You can ride that pony every day, and swim. And eat lots of barbecue. And then there's Fargo. Tucker and I know how you feel about Fargo…"

Brody chewed and swallowed. "But I told Dustin and Adam that we'd be home next week." The two boys,

Brody's best friends, lived down the street from them in San Antonio.

"You can call your friends and tell them you're staying here for the summer, after all, but that you'll be back as soon as school starts."

Brody wasn't going for it. "Mom. We were gonna build a tree fort in Dustin's backyard. I bet they've already started on it. And I'd miss soccer camp—and what about soccer practice? That starts at the *beginning* of August. And what about Disneyland? You said we could probably go to Disneyland, in July…"

Somehow, she hadn't expected all these objections. She saw now that she should have come at this a little better prepared.

She thought of Tucker's angry eyes, thought of what he'd have to say to her if she blew this, if she had to lay down the law and drag her son out to the ranch, sulking and surly the whole way. Since Tucker didn't trust her, he'd assume that somehow she'd poisoned Brody against the idea of a summer at the Double T. Good gravy, life got difficult when the father of your son had you branded as a liar.

And wait a minute…

She shouldn't be so negative. She should remember that her son was a reasonable kid and they could work this out between them. She reminded him, "I thought you liked it at Tucker's."

"I do. I like it a lot. And I've been a little sad, to think I won't see Fargo anymore." He blinked and added hastily, "And Tucker, too. I really like Tucker—but a tree house, Mom. And *Disneyland.*"

Shamelessly, she bargained, "You could build a tree house out at the ranch. And have the new friends you've made here at Gramma's out to visit whenever you wanted. I know they have soccer camp around here somewhere, too. We can arrange for you to go to that. And I don't see why we can't still go to Disneyland—" with Tucker, she reminded herself "—and Tucker might even want to go, too."

More chomping of Cheerios. Then, "I'd still miss the beginning of soccer practice, though..."

He sounded less resistant. Didn't he? She sipped from her coffee and answered him frankly, "Yes. I'm afraid you *would* miss a practice or two." She sipped some more, giving him time to think it over a little.

He slanted her a glance, looking so much like his father that he took her breath away. "Maybe I could invite Dustin and Adam to come visit me out at the Double T."

She gave him a slow smile. "You know. I'll bet that could be arranged. We'd have to talk it over with Tucker, though."

"Oh. Yeah. I mean, it *is* his house."

"Exactly."

Another bite of Cheerios. And then another. And finally, "Okay, Mom. Let's do it."

Relief poured through her. "Great."

He pointed his spoon at her. "Don't even think about it."

She sat back, widened her eyes. "What?"

"Rubbing my head and telling me you love me."

Busted. "But I do love you. I love you *so* much."

"I love you, too, but don't get all gooey, 'kay?"

"'Kay."

"And Mom?"

"Hmm?"

"Is Tucker, like, your boyfriend or something?"

She almost choked on her coffee. "Why do you ask?"

"Your face is red—well, except for the part that's all black and blue."

"You better watch it. I might just have to ruffle your hair, after all."

"That means you're not going to answer me, right?"

She drank more coffee.

He grunted. "You're not. And that prob'ly means he *is* your boyfriend. Right?" As she tried to compose an acceptable reply, one that would be honest and yet still not reveal the central truth that was Tucker's to tell him, he barreled right on, "Mom. It's okay if you have a boyfriend. I loved Dad and you loved Dad. A lot. But now Dad's in heaven and you're a widow and widows are allowed to have boyfriends. Especially the kind of boyfriend that gets along with their kids."

"You mean…a boyfriend like Tucker?"

Brody nodded. "And you know what? I think I need another bowl of Cheerios."

Lori set down the bottle of bug repellent after giving herself several protective squirts. Then she pulled another chair over, put her bare feet up on it and leaned back. She looked up at the stars and sighed.

It was nice, out by the pool. A slight breeze cooled her cheeks and a chorus of crickets trilled out their endless song and she could hear the water, softly lapping against the sides of the pool. Lightning bugs winked on and off across the lawn, tiny living lanterns in the darkness.

"So we're going to Disneyland next month." His voice came from behind her. It wasn't the warm, seductive voice she remembered from that other night, when they sat out here together and watched Brody and Fargo rolling around on the grass.

But it wasn't dangerous and hateful, either.

At least not *too* dangerous…

She decided to consider his tone a step in the right direction and sent a backward glance at his tall, broad-shouldered form. He stood at the edge of the brick path that led over from the South Wing.

"Have a seat," she suggested and lifted a hand toward the chair beside her.

Then she leaned back and shut her eyes to let him know that it wasn't a big thing to her, either way. He could stay, or he could turn and head back the way he had come. She'd be perfectly content, alone in the darkness with the cricket songs and the gold flashes of the lightning bugs.

Then again…

There *was* that tiny flicker, the thing called hope, bravely rising within her. Her heart was beating too fast and her breath had snagged in her throat—at the sound of his voice, at the sight of him standing there.

So maybe it *was* a big thing to her. She *did* want him to stay.

But he couldn't know that. And she was glad he couldn't. Though she'd sworn never to let another lie pass her lips, her response to him fell into that gray category labeled, *If he doesn't ask, I'm certainly not going to tell.*

She sensed rather than heard his approach. The chair beside her gently scraped the tiles. He dropped down next to her, close enough that she got a faint hint of his aftershave. His tanned bare arm—he wore chinos and a cream-colored polo shirt—brushed hers. She felt his warmth.

Acutely.

She lifted her head and looked at him. He seemed to be studying her bare feet. Slowly, his gaze tracked upward, over her legs and her light summer skirt, over her belly and her breasts, in a slow once-over that undressed her as it went.

He met her eyes. "Except for the black eye and the bandage, you're looking pretty healthy." The remark was heavy with innuendo.

She decided to ignore the innuendo—and go strictly with the words themselves. "Yes, I'm feeling pretty good, thank you. And you're right. We're going to Disneyland in late July. Or Brody is, with one or the other of us."

"Yeah. That's what Brody said." He looked at her steadily. Kind of hungrily, really—or maybe that was just a trick of the shadows, an illusion created by the waving light cast upward from the depths of the pool. Yes. A trick of the shadows…and her own yearning heart.

She found her mouth felt a little bit dry. She swallowed. "I had to do some convincing, to get him to come and stay here." She watched his brows draw together and rushed to explain herself. "Not that he didn't want to come. He did. But he had a lot of other plans, stuff lined up that he was looking forward to."

Tucker nodded. "Soccer camp. A tree house. Friends in San Antonio—and Disneyland. Or did I already mention that one?"

"You did. And I'm guessing he's laid it all out for you?"

"Pretty much. I got the idea he wanted me on the right page about his agenda, since he would be staying here."

"He's a smart guy."

"That he is."

"And *are* you—on the right page?"

"Yeah. I'd say I am."

"Well, good." She leaned her head back again. "I'll have to look into changing the plane reservations to California. And maybe you could see about ordering the boards and nails for the tree house."

"No problem. I'm thinking we've got what we need for the tree house already in one of the outbuildings by the stables."

"Great. I'll see if I can get the scoop on the local soccer camp, too."

He said, "I let Fargo sleep in his room."

She shut her eyes. "I can tell by your voice. That dog's in Brody's bed."

"I should have said no, then?"

She sighed. "A boy and a dog. What can you do?"

"That was pretty much how I saw it."

A pause. The chorus of cricket-song swelled all the louder. Somewhere in the trees, a bird trilled out, high and sweet. The song trembled on the air and then ended, the last note impossibly high, plaintive and lonely-sounding.

She could feel him watching her. His silence had a taut, breath-held quality. She dared to turn her head and look at him.

His dark eyes gleamed. He almost smiled—but no. He caught himself. He braced his hands on the chair arms. "Well. Good night, then." He rose and loomed above her.

"Good night," she said.

He turned for the brick path. She shut her eyes so she wouldn't have to see him go.

Saturday, Tucker and Brody started building the tree house in one of the oaks that rimmed the back lawn. Lori left them to it. She went into town and had lunch with her mother, who was sweet and affectionate—and wanted to know how things were going out at the ranch. Lori told her that Brody was having a great time.

And Enid asked the thousand-dollar question. "Does my grandson know, then, that Tucker's his dad?" Lori sighed and shook her head. "Honey, he has a right to know."

"I agree, but…" She blew out a breath and let the sentence finish itself.

Enid didn't look happy. "That boy needs to know."

"Mama. I'm aware of that."

"You'd better have a talk with Tucker, don't you think? We can't all just dance around the truth forever. It's not good. You, of all people, ought to know that by now."

When Lori returned to the Double T, Molly was just getting back from her Saturday shift at her salon, Prime Cut.

Tate's wife jumped from her red pickup and asked, "How are things workin' out?" Lori didn't quite know how to answer, since she hadn't a clue how much Tucker's sister-in-law knew. Molly gave her an understanding smile and helped her out a little. "I know that Brody is Tucker's son. Tucker told Tate—and Tate tells me everything. But you don't have to worry. Tate and I know how to keep our mouths shut."

Lori sighed. She'd been doing a lot of sighing lately. "Tucker doesn't want to tell Brody yet, so I guess we do need to keep a lid on it for now. It wouldn't be so great if Brody found out who his father is from some kid whose parents said too much in front of him."

Molly said pretty much what Lori's mother had said. "Brody seems like a levelheaded guy. Why not just tell him now?"

And Lori had to give her the same answer she'd given Enid. "It's Tucker's choice."

Molly wasn't buying that. "Well, it's the wrong choice if you ask me." Then she let out a low, infectious laugh. "Not that anybody did ask me." She leaned close to Lori and Lori got a whiff of her sexy perfume. "Listen. You need to talk, I'm here. Okay?"

"Thanks."

"And don't let Tucker push you around. Take it from one who knows. When it comes to these Bravo men, a woman has to stand tall and stand her ground."

Stand tall and stand her ground.

Lori kept waiting for the opportunity to do that. But Tucker gave her none. After that first night, when he joined her for those few too-brief minutes by the pool, he'd kept his distance when Brody wasn't around.

The days went by. Brody's friends came Monday, from San Antonio, for a five-day visit. They rode horses and swam in the pool and spent hours in the tree fort Brody and Tucker had built. Thursday night, they had three local boys over, too. They cooked hot dogs on sticks over an open fire and Tucker pitched a tent on the lawn, so the boys could camp out.

The local boys went home the next day at noon. At five, Dustin's mother came to take her son and Adam back to San Antonio. She had family in the Hill Country, so she and the boys would stay there over the weekend, to break up the long ride.

"I wish they didn't have to go," Brody said, as he and Lori stood in the driveway, waving goodbye, Fargo beside them. Brody added with a big smile, "But I sure did have a good time…" He ducked before she could ruffle his hair. And then he looked at her, suddenly solemn. "Mom. You okay?"

She started to tell him she was fine. And a voice in her head chided, *Remember. No lies.* "I'm okay," she said. It was true. Not great. Not particularly happy.

But okay. Getting by.

"You seem kinda sad…"

"Maybe a little."

"Because of Tucker?"

"What makes you think that?"

"I don't know…" His voice trailed off and she let that one go without a response. Then he asked, "Maybe you want to go home?"

She thought about that, about how much easier it would be, home in San Antonio, in her own house, living the good life she'd made for herself there, without Tucker around all the time—close, but so far away—reminding her constantly of all the ways she'd messed up. She confessed, "I guess I'm a little bit homesick. How about you?"

He frowned, thinking deeply. "Nope. I guess not. I kind of like it here."

"Then let's stay."

He gave her a grin. "Okay."

They turned for the house, Fargo right behind them.

Inside, Brody headed for the game room in the basement at the back of the house to play video games on the big-screen TV in there. Lori climbed the stairs to the bright, comfortable room Tucker had assigned her. She set to work at the little desk by the window, paying the bills she'd had forwarded from San Antonio, thinking as she wrote the checks that she was going to have to face Tucker down somehow, find a way to make him see that it was time to tell Brody who his real father was.

Tucker came home from the office and paused just inside the front door. The house was so quiet. He knew a moment of stark, echoing emptiness. The thought came to him: Lori and Brody were gone.

Impossible. She wouldn't dare…

And then Mrs. Haldana, who ran his wing of the house for him now, appeared from the dining room. "Ah. Mr. Bravo." She gave him her cool, professional smile.

He demanded much too gruffly, "Brody and his mother. Where are they?"

If his harsh tone disturbed the housekeeper, she didn't let on. "The boy is in the game room. Mrs. Taylor has gone upstairs."

He felt relief then, a warmth—and a kind of weakness—stealing all through him. "Thank you."

She nodded and went back the way she had come. He headed for the stairs in the utility room beyond the breakfast area, moving fast, needing, absurdly, to see for himself.

He found Brody right where the housekeeper had said he would. The kid sat cross-legged in front of the television playing some space-monster game. On the giant screen, a leering green creature exploded.

"Pow! Gotcha!" Fargo, stretched out at Brody's side, perked up his ears. The mutt turned his ugly head, thumped his tail on the carpet and whined in greeting. Brody slid Tucker a glance and kept on thumbing the controls. "Hey, Tucker—wanna play?"

Fargo got up and came over. Tucker scratched him behind the ears. "Later, maybe."

"'Kay…"

"Your mother upstairs?" As if he didn't already know.

"Guess so…"

Fargo flopped back down at Brody's side and Tucker turned for the stairs to the main floor. He walked fast, up the basement stairs and through the utility room. But once he got to the foot of the main staircase that would take him to the second floor, he slowed down. He went quietly, aware of each footfall, not wanting her to hear his approach and refusing to consider why that might be.

The door of her room was open, so he stopped there,

in the doorway. He stood very still and he watched her, heat and hunger curling low inside him.

He knew she wanted him, too. She'd told him so, flat out, that evening a week and a day ago now, when he'd finally confronted her with all of her lies, when he'd gotten her agreement to come here, to stay with him while he got to know the son she'd kept from him.

Yeah, he'd been avoiding her.

But as he stood in the doorway and watched her, he wondered why. What was the point? True, what she'd done was unforgivable.

He couldn't trust her.

But damn. He still had a powerful yen for her. They were living in the same house, for as long as he wanted it that way. Why should he spend his nights alone, longing for the feel of her, the warmth and softness and sweet, sweet scent of her? Why should he only imagine what it might be like, to reach for her, to feel her melt in his arms, to *taste* her—all of her?

Why should he lie awake taunted by memories of that one night so long ago?

Why deny himself? When he could have her now, when she'd told in no uncertain terms that she wanted him, too? Yes, she'd killed his tender, hopeful dreams of the life they might have shared. He knew now that all that had only been a fool's fantasy. But his desire for her? It was stronger than ever. Why the hell shouldn't he have her? Especially considering that denial only seemed to make his hunger for her stronger.

He watched as she turned in her chair, reached for a drawer in the desk, and spotted him from the corner of her eye. She went very still, slim arm stretched out, silky hair falling forward over her shoulder. He saw her catch her breath.

Then she straightened and spun the swivel chair around so that she faced him. "Tucker. I didn't..." Her sweet mouth trembled.

He studied her unforgettable face, the delicate features, the tempting plump mouth. Her left eye was no longer swollen. The bruises were fading, turning from the vivid purple of those first few days to a pale rainbow of yellows, greens and blues. She'd stopped wearing the bandage. The long cut at her temple, cross-hatched with stitches, looked angry and red.

He demanded softly, "You didn't what?" And he let his gaze wander lower, down her slim throat, where he could see the tiny pulse beating much too hard, over the snug top she wore and the fine, full breasts beneath it, to the smooth bit of skin that was visible between the top and her pink shorts. He admired the outward curve of her hips and after that, her bare legs, her slim, perfect ankles. He went all the way, to the tips of her pink canvas shoes and then, slowly, he tracked back up the way he had come until he was looking right into those startled blue eyes once again.

She swallowed. "I didn't know you were standing there."

With a shrug a damn sight lazier than the heat that blazed within him, he stepped across the threshold.

"Tucker?" she asked, her voice suddenly husky. She rose from the chair. "What are you doing?" He didn't answer. Not in words, anyway. He pushed the door shut behind him, finding the privacy lock by feel and twisting it. "Oh, Tucker…" She raised a hand, pressed the back of it against her mouth.

"Do you want me to go?"

Her hand dropped to her side. She swallowed again. And then, her gaze locked with his, her back straight and her chin high, she shook her head. "No." It came out in a whisper. "Please. Stay."

So he covered the distance between them and took her in his arms.

Chapter Thirteen

Tucker wrapped those big, strong arms around her and Lori was lost. Gone. Swept deliciously away. The high walls of hurt and anger between them were—at least for that moment—shattered to rubble, toppled by the force of their mutual need.

He kissed her, a punishing kiss...

At first.

But when she opened her mouth with a surrendering sigh, the kiss changed in an instant, grew wet and soft and so erotic. His tongue slid past her lips. Hot and slick, it swept the inside of her mouth, leaving her weak-kneed, clutching his big shoulders just to stay on her feet.

He lifted his head with a groan—and then slanted it

the other way, covering her lips again in a kiss so long and deep and slow that she thought she would die of the sheer pleasure of it. His hands, so warm and strong, roamed her back, sliding up under her little shirt, finding the clasp of her bra, expertly slipping the tiny hooks free. He ran a finger, oh-so-slowly, down the bumps of her spine, the teasing touch setting off hot flares as it went.

And then, with another low groan, he lifted his mouth from hers again. He looked down at her, dark eyes velvet-soft, face flushed, mouth swollen, as he brought his hands around to the front of her, slipping them up under her unclasped bra. She stared into his eyes and shuddered in delight as he covered her breasts with his two big, cupping hands. Her nipples drew up, hard and tight. He flattened his hands, rubbed his palms against them, until she moaned aloud.

And then he smiled at her. "Yeah," he said, and "yeah," again. His smile changed, became something darker. "I want to see you… I have to see you…"

He took the hem of her shirt and he pulled it up. She raised her arms and off it went. He hooked his fingers under the satin straps at her shoulders, lingering for a moment, hands stroking the tender skin of her upper arms as he brought those satin straps down. The bra slid low. He whipped it away.

"Lori," he whispered, lowering his big golden head. "Lori…" His lips closed over her aching nipple. He drew on it, nipped it with careful teeth, flicked it with his tongue.

And she surged up against him, clutching his shoulders, wishing in some vague, shattered sort of way that this magic, this pleasure, could bring them closer in the ways that really mattered. That somehow this white-hot delight they found in each other would help him come to trust her again.

It wouldn't, not really. And she did know that—in her head. Her heart and her body, though? They had different ideas.

As he suckled one breast, he took the other in his hand, cradling it, positioning it for his mouth, and then he claimed it. She speared her fingers in his brown-gold hair, let her head drop back and moaned aloud.

And then his hand moved lower, to the hook at the top of her pink shorts. She knew what he wanted and she helped him, unhooking it for him, sliding the zipper down, slithering out of the shorts as he shoved them over her hips. They dropped around her ankles. She lifted one foot and then the other and kicked the shorts away.

The panties came next. He pushed at them, slid his fingers beneath the delicate elastic, guiding them down. They caught on her shoes and tangled so tight she couldn't get free of them.

He left them there. He was too busy right then, his mouth at her breast, his hand on the curls between her thighs. He petted her, fingers combing, ruffling, and then, very gently, sliding lower, easing her open, dipping one finger into the slick, wet folds of her sex.

She lifted toward him, bucking her hips, lost now to everything but the feel of his mouth at her breast—and more than that, his hot touch at that hidden, oh-so-sensitive spot.

She was so wet, dripping. And her legs were shaking. She could feel herself rising, the pleasure spreading, fulfillment blooming, closer…closer. She didn't know if she could stay on her feet.

And then she didn't have to.

He was lifting her high against his chest. He took her mouth again as he carried her to the bed.

He set her down, carefully, on the jade-green coverlet, breaking the passionate kiss to tug her gently to the edge, so her legs hung over and her feet touched the floor. She reached for him, holding up yearning arms. But he didn't go down to her.

Instead, still fully dressed, he knelt at her feet and gently removed her hobbling, twisted panties. Her shoes were next. He took her right foot in one big hand and untied her shoelace with the other. She canted up on her elbows and looked down her own body, between her bare breasts, past the wet auburn curls at the top of her thighs and into his hot, dark, hungry eyes.

He slid that shoe off and set it aside and then he lifted her bare foot and kissed it. He nipped her toes, each one in turn, and she thought how truly lovely it was, to be a grown woman with him and not a scared virgin girl.

He kissed his way upward, teeth scraping against the vulnerable inner curve of her naked foot, his tongue licking, his lips planting little hot, swift kisses—on the muscles of her calf, the inner curve at her knee, the tender insides of her thighs.

Oh, and then…

He moved in closer, easing her legs over his shoulders. He spread his big hands on her thighs and with the tips of his fingers he opened her.

And then his tongue was there, licking, at first, then latching on, sucking so gently, drawing her to him.

So close, so close…

She fell back to the bed, moaning, and let her eyelids drift shut as he kissed her and licked her and she felt herself rising, higher and higher. She quivered on the brink.

And then she broke wide-open in a scatter of stars, a shower of light and sweetness, a taste like champagne on her tongue and the musky scent of her own desire all around her.

She heard herself crying, "Oh!" and "Yes!" and "Please…"

When she could think again—when she could *move* again, she reached down to try and pull him onto the bed with her.

But he sat back on his heels and shook his head. "I can't."

She pushed herself to a sitting position. "But why not?"

He reached out, stroked her thighs, brushed the reddish curls, lazily, possessively. "I didn't stop to get a condom…" His fingers dipped in—one and then another. She gasped as her inner muscles contracted around them. And then, so slowly, he took his hand from her, lifted it to his lips and licked her wetness off his fingers.

"Tonight," he said.

She nodded, mentally ticking off the hours until their son would go to bed. "Oh, yes."

He bent close again, put his mouth against her. His silky head pressed into her belly. She felt his tongue as it traced the slick groove, found that swollen nub, and flicked it maddeningly. She cupped the back of his head with her hand, groaning, pressing him even closer.

And then she couldn't stay sitting up for one more second. With a long sigh, she fell back across the bed. She clutched the coverlet in her two fists, and let out a cry of sudden, sharp wonder as she slammed against the peak again, crested it, went tumbling over. The world burst wide-open, and her body turned inside-out.

She felt the bed shift and opened her eyes.

Tucker was bending over her, one knee braced on the mattress. She reached for him again. He shook his head, whispered, once more, "Tonight..."

He lowered his head—keeping his body carefully away from her—and kissed her lips. She tasted herself on his tongue, for a too-brief moment, only. Too soon, he was lifting his mouth from hers, pausing to kiss the long, ugly scar on her temple....

And then he was pulling away, rising to stand by the side of the bed. He looked down at her. He still had all his clothes on.

And she? Except for one pink canvas shoe, she was naked, flung out across the bed, with not a shred of modesty. His eyes gleamed as his gaze swept over her. She felt no urge to cover herself, only a deeper kind of pleasure still—at the hot look of pure lust on his face, at the knowledge that tonight, there would be more.

Oh, yes. So much more...

It wasn't until several minutes later, as she stood in the shower washing the scent of her own arousal from her body, that she realized she'd let him get away without so much as a mention of the ever-present question: when was he going to be ready to tell their son what Brody needed to know?

But then, as the warm water poured over her, she smiled a woman's knowing smile. *Tonight,* he had said.

Once Brody was safely in bed, she would go to him. Or he would come to her.

Whichever. It didn't matter. The point was, they'd be together. They would make long, slow, tender love.

She would be with him, in his arms. And that meant she'd have ample opportunity to ask the question gently, and to get the answer she sought.

And there was more than that. Oh, yes, there truly was. There was that little flare of hope inside her, the one that had refused to die.

That tiny flare was a bright flame now.

Maybe. Just maybe, she and Tucker could find their way to each other, in the truest sense, after all.

For the first time since he'd learned that Brody was his son, Tucker Bravo was an inattentive father. A man is only human, after all. He only has so much attention to give at any specific time. And since those moments up in Lori's bedroom, all his attention was hard-wired directly on to the night to come. Remembered images kept flashing through his brain: Lori, naked on the bed, a rosy flush on her pale skin, that long red hair of hers spilled out across the green bedspread, those silky curls between her legs wet and glistening from his kisses.

He was useless. Hopelessly distracted. Waiting only

for the hour when Brody climbed into his bed and Lori—and the night to come—were his to take.

Getting through dinner. Now there was a challenge. He forked up food he hardly tasted and tried his damnedest not to let his gaze linger too long on the red-haired woman who sat across from him, looking so sweet and serene. She smiled indulgently at their son as Brody chattered away about his friends from San Antonio and his new buddies from town. Peter, one of the town kids, had invited him and the other two town boys to a sleepover tomorrow night.

"Can I go, Mom?"

She sent Tucker a look then, slightly questioning, including him in the decision. He shook himself and nodded and tried not to look at her mouth, not to think of her kisses and the way her body had moved under his hands, the way she had sighed and shuddered and pressed herself closer...

"Yes," she said to his son. "You can go."

Brody beamed. "Sweet. We'll sleep out, like we did when everyone was here. And Peter's dad will cook cheeseburgers and we'll tell scary stories and not freak out when we hear strange noises, not go running inside in the middle of the night like a bunch of big babies..."

Brody chattered on.

Tucker poked food into his mouth and nodded at what he hoped were the right places and counted the hours, the minutes, the *seconds* until bedtime—which was much too long in coming.

After the meal, Brody whipped Tucker's butt at the space-invader game. The fact that Tucker lost was nothing new. Brody usually beat him; a grown man didn't have a prayer against a kid when it came to a video game. But most times, Tucker could at least hold his own.

Not that night.

In his ten-year-old way, Brody was polite about cleaning Tucker's clock. "It's all right, Tucker. Maybe Sunday night, after I'm back from Peter's, we can play again. You might even get past level one before you totally wipe out. I could give you a few hints on strategy. But you would have to really listen, because you seem kind of, like, out of it tonight. You just can't be out of it when you play Alien Aggression—Tucker? D'ja hear me?"

He blinked a certain graphic erotic image of Lori from his mind and grinned at his son. "I heard you. Every word."

"Oh. Yeah. Sure. Right..." Brody waved a hand and flattened his lips—and something about the gesture and his expression reminded Tucker of Tate.

Mine, Tucker thought again, love and pride arrowing through him; love and pride and a fierce determination to be the kind of father he and Tate had never had: a *real* father, one who was there, every day, one who showed how much he cared. A dad a kid could turn to when things got tough.

Brody shook his head. "I've tried to be nice about it. But you got to face it, Tucker. You really sucked tonight."

"Hey!" Tucker assumed an expression of mock-outrage. "Don't be dissing me, man..."

Brody snorted. "It's not dissing you. It's just the truth."

"That does it." Tucker reached out, grabbed Brody and started tickling him.

Brody shouted—in laughter and surprise. They rolled together on the game room rug, Brody squirming, laughing, shouting, "No, stop, argh!" as Fargo ran around them in a circle, barking and wagging his long, wiry-haired tail.

When they rolled apart, panting, both of them laughing by then, Tucker looked up to find Lori standing over them. She braced her hands on her hips. "Having a good time, boys?"

Fargo plunked his skinny butt down and let out a final, gleeful bark. And Tucker and Brody looked at each other and laughed some more.

Brody went upstairs to take his bedtime shower at nine. As a rule, when he was ready for bed, he'd wander out of his room in his pajamas, sleepy-eyed, smelling of soap and toothpaste, his cowlick standing straight up at the back of his head. He'd say goodnight—usually to Tucker first and then to his mother.

That evening, Tucker waited in his study for Brody to come and find him. He spent the time staring blindly at his computer screen, pretending to play Spider Solitaire, but really long gone in fantasies of the night to come. Twenty-five minutes crawled by.

How damn long did a kid's shower take?

After thirty-one minutes, Tucker decided to find out why the hell Brody had chosen that night to be the cleanest kid in Texas. He shut down the computer and headed for the main stairs.

He found Lori in the upstairs hallway. She stood in the doorway to her room, leaning against the doorjamb, arms crossed beneath those breasts he intended to be kissing soon—and one foot crossed over the other, toe to the hardwood floor.

He wanted to grab her and haul her close, but somehow he restrained himself and muttered darkly, "He drown?"

Her eyes made promises he intended to see that she kept and one side of that soft mouth lifted in a teasing grin. "I knocked on his bathroom door a few minutes ago. He's still breathing, believe me. He's doing just fine."

"Doing *what?*"

"He's having a bath."

"But he likes a shower…"

"Every once in a while, he wants a bath. He'll sit in there for up to an hour sometimes, floating Lego boats, relaxing. He even sings while he's in there…" She cocked her head. "Listen…"

He strained to hear. His son's voice came to him— so young, slightly off-key. He recognized the song. "Yellow Submarine?" She nodded. "There's an oldie for you. Way before my time." He listened some more. "Sounds like he knows all the words."

"Henry taught it to him." She looked at him levelly, as if she dared him to say a word against her precious dead husband.

He tamped down his bitterness that she'd let some other man teach his son bathtub songs. As he'd already told her, whatever he thought of Henry Taylor personally, he was willing to admit that the man had done well by Brody.

And he didn't want to talk about her husband, anyway. He didn't want to talk, period.

He moved a step closer. And another. She didn't move back. Her scent came to him, warm and fresh and sweet, bringing memories of a night so long ago, of a young, eager girl, a girl he had called by her sister's name. Of a pink gown and a prom queen's crown and the armful of red roses they'd given her when they set that crown on her head.

Memories…

Of that night two weeks ago, when she wore pink again and he'd held her in his arms and told himself that his mind was playing tricks on him. She wasn't the same girl, the girl he would have given up the world for, if only he could have the right to hold her through all the nights to come—all the nights that were lost to him, as his son had been, for way too many years.

"Tucker…" She said his name softly—in warning? Or invitation? Or maybe a little of both? That tiny pulse was beating, a slight flutter, so tempting, at her long, white throat.

He lifted a hand. Again, eyes wide, mouth trembling, she held her ground. He touched her, laid the back of his index finger, lightly, against that beating pulse, felt it leap in response.

She shuddered and sighed, unable to hide her need for him, as he trailed that finger down along the silky flesh of her neck. He traced the wings of her collar-bones, slipping his finger beneath the soft cotton fabric of her top, feeling the straps of her bra, thinking that he would get it off her right away, the minute he had her alone in his room.

Alone, he thought. *Just the two of us…*

Beneath the zipper of his slacks, he was one long, hard ache. It was an ache made pleasurable by the sure knowledge of satisfaction to come. He spread his hand around her neck, clasping—lightly, carefully—thumb and middle fingers to either side, feeling again the agitated flutter of her pulse.

"Oh, Tucker…" She wasn't warning him now. And she was far beyond invitation. All the way to outright surrender…

Good, he thought. *Yes.*

He dipped his head a fraction closer to her uptilted mouth—but he didn't kiss her. Oh, no. Not yet. Her warm breath flowed across his cheek. Her breasts rose and fell, the rhythm agitated. Needful.

The silky waterfall of her hair flowed back over her shoulders. He took himself a handful of it—warm and alive and scented of her—and he brought it to his mouth, rubbed it against his lips.

Her control broke. With a low cry, she surged against him, offering her mouth.

He took it, smoothing the strands of hair out of the way, kissing her, spearing his tongue into the liquid heat beyond her lips. Her tongue came to meet him, sliding and slipping along his, tasting him as he tasted her.

He gathered her close, thinking way back in some still-rational corner of his mind that he needed to keep the brakes on. He couldn't afford to start tearing off her clothes. Brody might find them like this…

And then he forgot Brody. He worked his hips against her, his erection past an ache of pleasure now, so hard it was hurting, so hard that his mind spun with the need to open his fly, yank up her skirt, rip off her panties and bury himself deep in her silky heat.

Incredibly, through the dense, clinging fog of his own sexual hunger, he stayed just aware enough of where they were—and who was nearby. It came to him, vaguely, that Brody had stopped singing.

She must have noticed, too.

They pulled apart at the same time, he with a groan, she with a tiny cry of loss. He stepped back, so he wasn't touching her, though his senses clung to the remembered feel of her, soft and so willing, rubbing all along the front of him. His whole body burned.

Their eyes met, held. And then her gaze skittered on, past his shoulder, toward the door to Brody's room. She whispered, "It's okay. He's still in there…"

He started to reach for her again—and somehow stopped himself. He shut his eyes, took another step backward and swore beneath his breath.

She promised, so softly, "It won't be long now…"

He sucked in slow, even breaths. He counted to ten. Through sheer teeth-gritting will, he made his erection subside enough that it stopped tenting up the front of his slacks. He was barely in control again when he heard bare feet padding toward them.

Lori said, a little too brightly, "Well, Brody. Ready at last?"

"Yep. Came out to say g'night."

"Sleep tight," Lori said.

Tucker ordered his grimace into a smile and made himself turn. He tried to look easy and relaxed, raising a hand in a gesture midway between a salute and a wave—a *casual* gesture, he sincerely hoped. "See you tomorrow, big guy."

Brody frowned, cowlick on alert, sharp eyes tracking—Tucker to Lori, back to Tucker again. "You guys look weird. What's going on?" And then, very slowly, he grinned. "Okay. I get it. It's a boyfriend and girlfriend thing, huh?"

A definite snorting sound escaped Lori. "No comment, mister. Get to bed."

Still grinning, Brody turned and left them alone.

Chapter Fourteen

As soon as Brody shut his bedroom door behind him, Tucker grabbed Lori's hand. "Let's go."

Lori didn't hesitate. Every nerve humming, she followed him downstairs to the master suite, to his beautiful bedroom, with its maroon walls and soft recessed lighting. The steel-blue duvet on the king-size bed was already turned down—by the capable hands of Mrs. Haldana, no doubt.

Tucker wasted no time getting her out of her clothes. Off went her shirt and away went her bra. He kissed her, a hard, quick kiss, and then he took away the skirt she'd put on that afternoon after her shower. She stepped free of it and he tossed it on a chair. She kicked off her sandals, shoved down her panties.

And there she was, standing in front of him without a stitch on.

Strange how very natural it seemed, to be naked with him. He took her shoulders, so gently, and smiled into her eyes.

She reached for his belt.

He let her undress him, let her slide the belt off and away, lifting his big arms so she could push his shirt up over his gorgeous washboard belly and his deep chest. He stepped back and sat on the edge of the bed and she knelt and took off the soft leather mocs he liked to wear around the house. Grinning, she stood, grabbed his hand, pulled him upright again, and got rid of his cargoes and the boxers beneath them.

When at last he was as naked as she, they stood facing each other, bathed in the muted light from above. She thought how very beautiful he was, a fully mature man now, broader and more imposing than she remembered him from that long-ago night, his body filled out, the muscles so strong and hard, along his arms, at his chest, down his ridged stomach and his powerful thighs. His manhood jutted, eager and ready, from the dark nest of hair at his groin.

Another smile quirked the corners of his mouth. "At last."

In complete agreement, she sucked in a long breath and nodded. He offered his hand. She took it. It was only a step or two back to the bed.

He guided her down and rose above her, straddling her. He stroked her body, slow, arousing caresses, all along the length of her.

And he lowered his mouth and he kissed her—first her lips and then lower. And lower still…

Until, once again, she was tossing her head on the pillows, pleading sounds rising from her stretched-back throat, as his endless, intimate kiss worked its special magic, until her body shimmered and shook and her mind flew away and there was only sensation, a rolling, sparkling river of it, flowing all through her, out along every quivering nerve.

She called his name as she went over and she was still shaking with the wonder of it when he slid up her body and reached for the drawer in the night table.

"Oh," she cried. "Let me…let me…" She took the condom from his hand and tore the wrapper off. Then she wrapped her fingers around him, squeezing, sliding her hand up, over the silky head where a drop of moisture clung, and down to the thick base jutting from that wiry nest of hair—and slowly back up again.

He caught her wrist, spoke through gritted teeth. "Just…do it. Put it on. Now, or I'll lose it…"

She obeyed, sliding the sheath over the thick, hot length of him. He straddled her once more. She guided him to her.

Her body took him—all of him—in one smooth, even glide. He settled between her cradling thighs, bracing his forearms on the pillows, tangling his hands in the wild spill of her hair.

"So sweet," he muttered. "So wet and hot and sweet…" He whispered her name, hoarse and low, and then he buried his head against her shoulder.

She wrapped her legs around him. They moved together, the rhythm changing and then changing again. All the while the pleasure was building, the world falling away to nothing. Now, at last, it was only the two of them—no anger, no hurt, no wrongs to be righted.

Just a woman and a man, fitted perfectly together, sharing a rolling, hot pleasure that built to fever pitch and then spun out, hovered on the edge of a vast darkness—and burst wide-open, lighting the night in a shower of stars.

They rested, but not for long. He couldn't stop touching her, kissing her, pressing himself tight to her willing body.

And she touched him, too, every sleek, hard inch of him. She kissed him—all of him. She pushed him to his stomach and she licked the sweat from the small of his back, her hand caressing, sliding over his lean waist and under him, until she clasped him with a greedy cry and he rolled to face her with a deep, hungry moan.

That time, she took the top position. She slid down onto him slowly, gathering him in by aching degrees. Once she had all of him, they moved together lazily, like waves lapping a smooth, sandy shore.

In the end, she collapsed on top of him and he gathered her close. She felt the deep, strong beating of his heart against her ear as fulfillment claimed her all over again.

After that, he settled the gray satin sheet over them and pulled her close to his side. She rested her head on his shoulder, feeling limp and wonderful and thoroughly satisfied, safe in the circle of his arms.

He pressed his lips against her hair and whispered, "We should do this more often. I'd suggest at least a dozen times a day."

She snuggled closer. "Excellent idea—though Brody could get a little lonely, if we're always off in a bedroom somewhere, with the door locked."

"Brody..." She could hear the smile in his voice. He stroked her shoulder, trailed a finger lightly down her arm. She made a low, pleasured noise and smiled to herself, feeling like a purring cat. And he asked, "What do you think he meant by that last remark tonight—the one about you and me and a 'boyfriend and girlfriend thing?'"

She shrugged and ran her hand over the sculpted contours of his chest. Dark hair grew across his pectoral muscles and down the center of his belly. She followed that silky trail, out to each side and then down along his solar plexus...

He caught her hand before she could go too low. "Watch it."

"I'd rather *feel* it."

He laughed then, a low, sexy laugh. "Lori Lee. You are definitely all grown up now."

"That's right." She nipped his earlobe and made a growling sound.

He turned his head and kissed her nose. "But seriously. Brody thinks you're my girlfriend?"

She tipped her head back so she could meet his eyes. "Kids can surprise you, the things they pick up on. And I suppose I *am* your girlfriend—as of now, anyway, aren't I?" She asked the question and then her heart skipped a beat as she realized she wasn't sure she wanted to hcar his answer.

What if he said no? What if he told her that the last thing he needed was a liar like her for a girlfriend? What if he said flat out that just because he'd had sex with her didn't mean she had any kind of claim on him?

And then she caught herself. Well, if he said that, so be it. Better to find out now. Bctter to get the painful truth right out there. Truth, after all, was the best way. She knew that from firsthand experience.

He didn't answer for the longest time. Finally, he said, "Yeah. I guess, from Brody's perspective, that you're now my girlfriend."

It was hardly what she'd hoped for—but not nearly as bad as she'd feared. "So, all right then." She was proud of how matter-of-fact she sounded. She lowered her head to his shoulder again. "There you have it."

"But how the hell did he know it, that's what I'm wondering? Until today, we haven't been near each other. And he's never said a word before to me, about the two of us."

"He's smart and observant, that's all. He sensed that we're, um, attracted to each other."

He tipped her chin up. "Has he said anything to you about it?"

She recalled that conversation at her parent's breakfast table the week before. "Yeah. He has."

"What?"

"The day we moved in here, when he and I talked it over, he did ask if you were my boyfriend."

"And you told him?"

"I didn't. I said nothing. I let him draw his own conclusions."

His eyes darkened in disapproval. "Why?"

She pushed at his chest until he released her, then she moved back to her own side of the bed and canted up on an elbow. "Think about it. You and I were hardly speaking then, but he'd seen us together before—that night he and I came over here, and at Lena's wedding. He knew there was *something* going on."

"So you lied to him."

"No. I just kept my mouth shut." She realized about then that this was the moment—the time to talk about the necessity of telling Brody the truth. "Tucker, even to a ten-year-old, it's a little odd, that we just moved right in with you. And you had me sworn to secrecy about what was really going on. So Brody explained the situation to himself by deciding it must be about you and me, since neither of us explained to *him* that you happen to be his father."

Tucker searched her face, and then he gave her one of those regal, overbearing, Ol' Tuck-style nods of his. "All right. Now that you've told me a little more about it, I understand your reasoning."

Irritation sizzled through her. "Oh. Well. Thank you very much."

"Lori. Come on…" He reached for her. She saw desire kindling in his eyes—and behind it, the deeper need to avoid the subject at hand.

She moved back. "No. Not now." She schooled her voice to a level tone. "Look. I agreed, at first, to wait until you were ready to tell him. But it's been a week since we moved in here, almost two weeks since you've known that he's your son."

"A week—two weeks—it's nothing."

"No. That's not so. Two weeks is long enough. It's *too* long. Brody adores you. It's not like you need the chance to win him over or anything. He's crazy about you. And it's long past time—years past time—that he got to know you as his father."

Tucker sat up, hooked his arms around his knees and muttered to the far wall, "Whose damn fault is it, that he doesn't know who I am? It's not *my* fault, Lori."

"Wonderful," she said under her breath. Dragging herself to a sitting position, she drew the sheet up to cover her breasts. "You want to play the blame game, okay. As I've said any number of times already, the fact that you didn't know your son for all those years is *my* fault. I accept that. I *own* it. And whether you believe it or not, I am paying every day for the truth that I kept from you— for the father that I kept from our son. So yes. For over ten years, it was *my* fault that Brody didn't know you. But for the last two weeks? Uh-uh. That's all on you.

"And you're right, it's only two little weeks. But it's two little weeks that we've all—you and me and my mom and dad and Tate and Molly—all of us, have been, in the strictest sense, lying to him. Lying, as you well know, didn't work for me at all. I've had up-close and personal experience with the damage lying can do. And I just don't want to do it anymore." He glanced back at her then. She saw pain in his eyes—and fear, too. And she found all her carefully controlled irritation with him draining away. "It will be okay," she said, softly now.

He swore and turned away from her and stared at the far wall once again. "What if he hates me? Damn it, he's happy. A happy kid. He thinks of your husband as his dad. He could so easily resent me for trying to take your husband's place."

She looked at his broad back and wanted to touch him, a touch of reassurance, of support. But she sensed he wouldn't want her hand on him, not right then. She tucked the sheet up higher under her arms and folded her hands on her thighs. "First of all, you're not going to be taking Henry's place. You have your *own* place in Brody's life, a very important place. And I do know Brody. Pretty darn well. I don't think he's going to resent you or hate you. He may not fall all over you, not at first. He usually likes to take his time about things, to think them over, to get used to them. But eventually, he's going to be glad to know what you mean to him, to build a relationship with you, to have you there to help him grow up."

"What if you're wrong?"

She knew she wasn't. But she'd already told him that. "If I'm wrong, we take it one day at a time. If he's angry for some reason to learn what you are to him, then we'll deal with it. He'll get past it. We all will."

Tucker still wouldn't look at her—but his next words had her heart lifting. "You'll be there. With me. When I tell him?"

"Of course, if you want me there."

"I'll need you there. In fact, I think it's only fair that you be the one to tell him."

"Fair?"

"Okay, wrong word. I think it's a good idea if you're the one who tells him. You're his mother and it'll be easier to take coming from you. You tell him. And then *I'll* tell him that—hell, I don't know—that I'm happy to have him for my son. Then, after that, *he* can tell *me*…whatever he needs to tell me."

She dared to draw in a deep, relieved breath. They really were getting somewhere, at last. "Agreed. We'll tell him together."

"But you'll break the news."

"That's right. And you can feel free to chime in any time you get the urge."

"Thanks," he said dryly.

"And we shouldn't put it off. Not for even one more day."

"Why did I know that was coming?"

"Tomorrow. It's Saturday. You won't have to rush off to the office. He's not going over to Peter's till the afternoon. We'll tell him at breakfast. There'll be plenty of time to talk."

Tucker turned his head again and looked at her over his shoulder. "All right. Tomorrow at breakfast." His bleak expression said he'd rather do just about anything else—eat scorpions, maybe. Go skydiving without a parachute…

"Tucker, it has to be done. And it *will* work out. Just watch."

The next morning, as planned, once they all three had their food and were seated at the table, Lori began explaining to her son that he had a father he didn't know about.

Before she actually got to the part about *who* that father was, her son set down his cereal spoon. "Wait a minute. I had another dad...before Dad?"

From the chair opposite Lori at the round breakfast table, Tucker shot her a look, one that warned, *Don't blow this or there will be hell to pay.*

Lori gave her son's father a wide smile. She was going for perky, for I-know-what-I'm-doing-here. But it didn't come off. Either Tucker didn't get the message or he simply didn't buy it; his dark expression didn't change.

She turned Brody's way again. Her son had not picked up his spoon. His wide brown eyes asked a thousand questions. She plowed ahead. "I guess maybe you don't remember the time before Henry, when it was just you and me?"

Brody frowned. "I don't know. I don't think so."

"Well, you were very little. I started dating Henry when you were two and we got married when you were barely three. But before I married him, you and I had a talk about your, er, natural father..."

Brody sat back in his chair. He was still frowning. "Mom. You just said I was hardly even three. I don't remember much from when I was three."

"That's fine. That's okay. But the truth is, a long time before Henry, there was someone...special. Someone I really, um, loved, and one night he took me to a dance and, well, we made you."

"At the dance?"

She blinked. "No. Later, actually."

"Oh."

"But where that happened isn't the point."

"It's not."

"No, the point is that we *did* make you. And then he had to go away and he never knew about you and I couldn't find him to tell him about you and then I met Henry and—"

"Mom."

"Um, yeah?"

"You don't look so good. Are you okay?"

"Yeah. Oh, yeah. It's just…this is hard, you know?" She could not look at Tucker. She knew if she did, she would burst into tears.

Oh, she'd been so sure she would know how to do this. Wrong.

Brody's frown deepened. "Are you saying that Dad wasn't *really* my dad?"

"Well, I—"

"Wait!" Brody's frown had vanished. He sat forward, shoulders curved to the table edge, chin jutting over his heaping bowl of Cheerios, suddenly eager, eyes alight. "I get it. It's like Dustin. He has his first dad. And then his mom got married again and that's his second dad, his stepdad. Two dads. So you're saying I'm, like, a two-dad kid?"

Thank God for smart children. "Yes. Yes, that's exactly what I'm saying."

The bright eyes narrowed. "But then, what about my first dad?"

And Tucker spoke at last, low and a little bit raggedly. "That would be me."

There was a silence the like of which Lori had never known. And then her son looked at Tucker sideways. "*You*, Tucker? You're my first dad?"

Tucker's Adam's apple bounced as he swallowed. "That's right. I'm your first dad."

Brody picked up his spoon. "Well." He paused, considered—and finally asked, "Should I call you that, then? Dad?"

Tucker wore the pained, stunned expression of a man in way over his head and not likely to be rising above adversity soon. "Uh. Call me Dad?"

"Yeah. Should I?"

"Do you want to?"

More considering on Brody's part. Then, "Yeah. I guess so. A dad should be called Dad. That's what I think."

Tucker gulped again. "Then you should. You should call me Dad."

"Okay, Dad." Brody nodded, a slow nod, as if, after careful reflection, he was certain that the right decision had been made. Then he shoveled up a big spoonful of cereal and stuck it in his mouth.

Chapter Fifteen

"Telling him went pretty well, I thought," Tucker said that afternoon. They sat at the edge of the pool in their swimsuits, with their feet in the water. Brody had already been dropped off at Peter's house.

Lori slid off the edge, kicking lazily, turning and bracing her forearms on the smooth tiles that rimmed the water. She rested her chin on her folded hands, felt her hair fan out and float around her. "I have to admit, though, it was touch-and-go there at the first."

He looked down at her, flashes of sunlight reflecting off the water's surface, gleaming in his eyes. "You should have seen your face when he asked you if we *made* him at the prom."

"Ouch. Big oops on putting my foot right in that one."

"But you managed to slide on by it."

"Yes, I did." She gave him her cockiest smile. "And aside from that—and a few other slightly rocky moments, it did go well. Which I said it would, if you remember…"

"How could I forget, with you right here to rub it in?"

She moved her elbow enough to nudge his bright orange board shorts—and the rock—hard thigh beneath them. "Just admit it. I know what I'm talking about."

He tipped his head to the side and looked at her through lazy-lidded eyes. "Maybe. Sometimes…"

"*Sometimes?* Hah!" She pushed back off the edge with one hand—and then splashed him a good one with the other.

"Hey!"

"Not *sometimes. Most* times, and don't you forget it—and there's water dripping off your nose."

"That does it."

"Don't even try it." Laughing, she shoved off with both feet as he fell forward, diving from where he sat.

She wasn't fast enough. He shot to the surface beside her, put his big hand on her head and pushed. She shrieked—an ear-piercing sound, cut off by necessity as she sucked in a breath before going under.

When she broke the surface, laughing and splashing, he grabbed for her. She shrieked some more and fanned up a hard blast of water to keep him at bay. It didn't work. He caught her by the wrist.

"Stop that. Let me go."

"Not a chance." He dragged her to him, hooked an arm around her and headed for the shallow end.

She found her feet. "Okay, okay. You win. Let me go."

"Uh-uh." He hauled her close, wrapped both big, wet arms around her and lowered his tempting mouth to an inch above hers. "Kiss me."

She pushed at his chest—though not very hard. "I should kiss you…because?"

His smile was slow and much too sexy. "Because you like it?"

She stopped pretending to struggle and made a big show of thinking that one over. "Hmm. Well, there is that…"

"Because your heart's beating harder and your breath is caught in your throat?"

"Now, how did you know that?"

He took her right hand, guided it down so that her palm lay over his heart. "Easy. Feel that?" She did. Oh, she really, really did. He commanded again, "So kiss me."

She pressed her spread hands against his chest—just enough to keep their lips from meeting. "You know, anybody who looked out a back window could see us from the house."

"Brody's not home. And anyone else is either one of the twins, too young to even *be* looking—or else old enough to know that they *shouldn't* be looking."

"Well." She licked her lips, on purpose, just to tease him. "I suppose an innocent little ol' kiss wouldn't hurt anyth—"

His mouth swooped down before she could finish.

Heaven. Absolute heaven. She wrapped her arms around his neck and gave herself up to the glory of that kiss—until his hand strayed up her back to the clasp of her suit top. Then she shoved him away.

"Tucker Bravo. I am not going topless in the Double T swimming pool."

He caught her hand. "How about my bedroom? Will you go topless there?"

She pulled free, put her index finger against her chin and made a prim face. "Hmm. Well, now, let me think about that…"

He swore. Then he grabbed her hand again and forged for the steps that led out of the pool, hauling her along behind him.

"Oh, my." She faked innocence for all she was worth. "Where are you taking me?"

He pulled her up the steps and out of the water. "Guess."

She didn't need to guess. Laughing, dripping water as she went, she let him drag her where she wanted to go. Fargo, basking in the shade of a patio umbrella, scrambled to his feet and hurried after them.

The lazy summer days went by. They were good days, Lori thought. Beautiful, happy days. Good days, followed by hot, sexy nights in Tucker's bed.

Brody stuck with his decision to call Tucker Dad. He slipped into his life as Tucker's child with no apparent transition period, no slightest sign of anger or resentment, no shyness about it and a total lack of wariness.

Tucker said he found that amazing.

Lori wasn't the least surprised. Her son had a true pragmatic streak. The father he'd known and loved was gone. It didn't bother him at all to find he had a spare— a long-lost dad who was absolutely, stone-gone crazy about him. A *fun* dad who sometimes *almost* could beat him at Alien Aggression. A dad who hung on his every word and said right out loud that Fargo could be Brody's now, too.

And then there were the gifts. Now it was out in the open that Brody was Tucker's, Tucker seemed determined to buy their son every video game, electronic gadget and overpriced toy known to man.

"Tucker," she told him when they were alone. "Brody doesn't need a Playstation, an X-Box *and* the latest version of Nintendo."

"No, but he *wants* them."

"I'm saying that one game system will do."

He gave her one of those puzzled man-style frowns, the kind of frown that proves men truly are from another planet. "But there are some games you can only play on one system or the other."

"So? He doesn't *need* every darn game there is."

"I thought I just told you. It's not about need."

She suppressed a sigh and tried to come at it from another angle. "You know, it's not always the best idea for a kid to get something just because he wants it. They start thinking they're entitled. They grow up with no concept of working for what they want, of waiting for it."

"Well, I can relate to that. Who wants to wait? Not me. If possible, I want what I want and I want it *now*." He reached for her.

She stepped back—several steps, actually. "And sometimes you don't get what you want."

He slanted her a dark look. "Is this about you and me?"

She blew out a breath. "No. This is about our son. About the things it's our duty to teach him—things like how *things* aren't everything."

Tucker shook his head. "Wow. That was a mouthful."

"I just don't believe you're not following me on this. I don't believe you can't see that it's not a good idea for a kid to have every toy or device he ever wanted just dropped in his lap."

"Maybe you're right."

She cast a glance heavenward. "Thank you."

But he was already smiling his slow, sexy smile. "Give me a break-in period, will you? Let me go hog-wild in a frenzy of outrageous and disgusting consumerism. Just for a while…"

When he looked at her like that she lost the ability to say no to him. "Oh, all right. But think about cutting back a little, okay?"

He put up a hand, like a witness swearing an oath. "I promise. Now get back over here and let me take off your clothes."

The next day, he had a three-thousand-dollar bicycle delivered to the house while he was at the office. Lori saw the price on the invoice the delivery man handed her. That bike had more gears than a semi truck.

"I'm going riding, Mom. I'm going riding right now!"

"Not on the highway," she warned. The state highway ran by at the end of the long, curving driveway.

Brody promised, "Just the driveway and the roads around the stables and stuff."

He put on the Day-Glo green and metallic-purple helmet that came with the bike, climbed on, and spent two hours racing out to and around the stables and up and down the driveway.

Lori told herself that a bike—even a grossly overpriced one—was a definite improvement over yet another video game system. And at least Tucker had shown the good sense to throw in a helmet.

Brody started soccer camp the second Monday in July. The camp went all day, five days a week for two weeks. After that, in the last week of July, they had the trip to Disneyland scheduled. Lori had fixed it so they could fly out of Dallas and Tucker had cleared his calendar. She'd bought him a ticket, too. Everything was arranged.

Thursday, Brody's fourth day at camp, Lori dropped him off in his soccer gear, with his ball and gallon-size insulated water bottle. Then she headed to Lena and Dirk's house to see her sister. The honeymooners had arrived home a few days before.

Lena was glowingly happy, with a golden tan. She fussed over Lori's still-healing injury and dragged her around the house so she could get a look at the new drapes and the bathroom tile and fixtures—all installed under their mother's conscientious supervision while Lena was away. Then they sat down in Lena's sunny new kitchen for coffee.

Lena chattered away about her honeymoon. "Boy, there is nothin' like a tropical island to make a person feel romantic—those balmy breezes blowing, maybe a pretty pink drink or two…oh, my goodness. What a time we had."

"I'll bet you did."

"And what about you and Tucker? You know, it's all over town that you and Brody are staying with him."

In the Junction, folks talked. You had to expect that. "I guess I'm not surprised."

"Everybody's wondering what's going on with you and Tucker. I let 'em wonder. I don't say a word."

"How did I get so lucky to have such a terrific sister?"

"That's a question you should ask yourself often. And does Brody know yet that Tucker's his dad?—aha! You're still smiling. That would be a yes, wouldn't it?" Lori nodded. Lena asked, "Brody take it okay?"

"Yep. Everything's going great."

"Everything?" Lena wiggled her eyebrows.

"Well…"

Lena let out a whoop of joy and pointed at Lori. "Look at that! That's a blush if I ever saw one. So I'm right, huh? You and Tucker are in love."

In love…

The two simple little words came out of her sister's mouth—and Lori realized they were absolutely true. She'd gone beyond hoping things might somehow work out. Now she was certain: she loved Tucker Bravo. And she wanted a life with him.

"So when's the wedding?" Lena had the ball and she was headed for the end zone. "Oh, honey. It's going to be so great. Mama and me will get right on it, because, really, it should be soon, don't you think? After all, I mean, you two have a ten-year-old son. Your wedding is long overdue. I want to help you pick your colors—you will let me, now won't you? You must admit, I always had an eye for color. And then, of course, you'll be closing up that house in San Antonio and moving home forever at last. Oh, I am so excited, I can barely—"

Lori stopped her with a laugh. "Whoa. Hold on. I think maybe I ought to talk to Tucker about all this first."

Lena waved a hand. "Oh, well. I suppose so. But make it quick, will you? We've got a wedding to plan."

All that afternoon and into the evening, Lori planned how she would say the words that night when they were alone. They were only four *little* words: *Tucker, I love you.*

It should be easy. Piece of cake. Like rolling off a log…

Still, her palms got sweaty and her heart went knocking hard against her ribs whenever she imagined herself getting those simple words out.

After dinner, Tucker and Brody went down to the game room for another extended session of zapping aliens, raiding sacred tombs and killing bad guys with digital six-guns in the video-game version of *High Noon.* Lori smiled to herself as they disappeared down the back stairs—and made a mental note to tell Tucker that his next gift to Brody should be a book, for crying out loud.

And then she thought, *I love you, Tucker,* and her pulse set to pounding like drums in the jungle and her mouth felt dust-bowl dry.

Wouldn't you know Brody would choose that night to take one of his baths? It was his longest bath ever, or at least, it seemed that way to Lori. He sang every song the Beatles wrote, one after another, from "All My Loving" to "Let it Be."

By the time he finally emerged to say good-night, Lori had decided that she could live the whole rest of her life without hearing one more song by George, Paul, John or Ringo.

"Love you, Mom."

"Good night. Love you, too."

"Night, Dad—don't forget."

"I won't. Good night."

Yawning, Brody wandered back to his bedroom and shut the door.

Lori turned to Tucker. "Forget what?"

Tucker put a finger to his lips, took her hand and led her down the stairs. By the time they got to his bedroom, she really didn't care what it was Brody didn't want Tucker to forget.

She was too busy realizing that this was it; time to tell him what was in her heart.

They undressed and got into bed and Tucker pulled her close, spoon-fashion, her back to his warm, broad chest, his thighs cradling hers. Heaven, she thought, as she did so often lately where this man was concerned. He ran a lazy finger down the length of her arm, and then twined his fingers with hers.

Time to say it. Time to just get it right out there.

She opened her mouth to tell him. But before she spoke, he nuzzled her ear and said, "Brody wants us to get married. I do, too."

Chapter Sixteen

Joy poured through her, bright as sunshine, sparkly as a thousand stars. She turned in his arms, lifted her mouth.

Tucker kissed her. She thought it was about the sweetest kiss they'd ever shared. When he raised his head it was only to whisper, "Did I just hear a yes?"

She wrapped her arms tighter around his neck. "Oh, Tucker. I do love you so. I love you with all of my heart."

Wow. She could hardly believe it. She'd said it. It was out. And it was easy as licking ice cream off a spoon. She shut her eyes with a sigh and waited to hear him say he loved her, too.

He kissed her nose. "Good. Then let's get married. Let's do it right away. We can fly to Vegas this weekend and get it done."

Get it done. He sounded like that comedian, Larry the Cable Guy, from the Blue-Collar Review comedy show. *Git 'er done,* Larry said, and everyone laughed.

Lori wasn't laughing. And the sparkles and sunshine had faded a little. She asked in a small voice, "Get married...because Brody wants us to?"

He gave her one of his men-are-from-Mars frowns. "Well, yeah—and I want it, too. We get along great, you and me. And most important, I think it's the right thing, the best thing, for Brody."

He's right, she told herself. *We do get along. And it probably is the best thing for Brody...*

But damn it. That just wasn't enough.

He must have read her thoughts by her expression—or at least their general drift. "All right. What's the problem?" Gently, she eased herself free of his arms. "What the hell did I do?" He sounded way too gruff—and too defensive.

She thought that he knew exactly what he'd done—or, to be more specific, what he *hadn't* done. She sat up and tugged at the sheet until it covered her. "So. Brody wants us married. And that's a good enough reason for you, huh? Well, I guess that makes sense. I mean, Brody wants a new game system, Brody gets it. Brody wants your dog—Brody gets it. Brody wants us to be married and there's no reason to even discuss it. Because whatever Brody wants, Brody gets."

He sat up beside her, his brow beetling in an impatient frown. "Listen. Brody's not the only one who wants this. *I* want this—I want *you*."

"You *want* me." She was certain he was being purposely dense.

"Yeah. I want you. You want me. We're both single and we have a son together, a son who'd like his parents to be married, a son who doesn't need to spend the rest of his childhood shuffling back and forth between here and San Antonio."

She folded her hands in her lap. "Tucker. I said I love you. I meant it. Now I'd really like to know. Do you love me?"

There was a silence. A great, big, fat, ugly one. Then he grumbled, "Look. I don't know about love. Not anymore."

Very carefully, she repeated, "Not anymore?"

"That's right."

"Not since…" She let the sentence trail off so he could finish it. And then, as he sat there glaring at her, not saying a word, she *knew*. She knew and she could hardly believe she hadn't realized before.

But then again, everything had been so good between them. So tender and sweet and open and loving…

Or had it?

Just because he took her to his bed, just because he treated her kindly, just because he could laugh and joke with her, she'd assumed that meant he'd put the past behind him.

She'd assumed too much.

She'd got it all wrong.

The healing scar at her temple pounded. Her stomach had tied itself into a hard tangle of knots. And he still hadn't spoken.

She spoke for him. "I kept your son from you. And you can't forgive that. You can't forgive it—and so you can't love me."

His eyes were a thousand miles deep, every one of them empty. "This is stupid. It's all just words, anyway. You say you love me. And I want to marry you. It looks pretty damn simple to me."

She stared down at her hands. They were folded so tight, the knuckles were white. She shook her head. "Oh, Tucker. I've had this all wrong. I'm so sorry…"

"Prove it. Marry me."

She raised her head, met those dark, fathomless eyes. "No. No, I really can't marry you." She lifted the sheet, turned to slide from the bed.

He caught her shoulder, strong fingers digging in. "You mean you won't."

She realized he had it right. And she nodded. "That's right. I won't."

"Because I won't say I forgive you. Because I'm not laying on the pretty words of love…"

"It's not about the words. I think you know that. It's about what's in your heart for me—or what's not."

"You blame me because I won't—"

"No. I don't blame you for anything. I did something you can't forgive. I didn't understand that before, how deep your anger with me goes. But now I think I do. Take your hand off me, please." His strong fingers squeezed tighter. She winced. "Let me go," she said, each word strong and final, leaving no doubt that she meant it.

His hand dropped away. She threw back the sheet,

got up and began gathering her scattered clothes. Once she had them on, she made herself face him. "Good night."

"So what now?" He just wouldn't leave it—not even for the night.

Fine. "Tomorrow I'll have a long talk with Brody. I'll explain that I love him—and *you* love him. But that you and I don't love each other the way married people do. Then I'll go home to San Antonio. Brody can stay till the end of the summer, just as we agreed when he and I first moved in here. When I come back to get him at the end of the August, we'll discuss where he'll stay when."

"I can't believe you're willing to do this to him."

And *she* couldn't believe how much he looked and sounded like Ol' Tuck at that moment. But she didn't say that. Trading insults, after all, wouldn't make things right between them. At that particular moment, she doubted that anything could. "Good night," she said again, and turned from him.

That time, he didn't say—or do—anything to stop her.

Chapter Seventeen

"But Mom. I thought you liked Dad. You said, when you told me he *was* my dad, that you *loved* him, even when you were young."

"I did," Lori said wearily. "I do." It was five in the afternoon and they sat in the kitchen, Brody smelling of soap and shampoo from his after-soccer shower, looking way too much like his father had the night before—as if he was going to grab her and shake her until she came to her senses and did what *he* wanted her to do. "I like Tucker—I *love* him—a lot. But we're not getting married and you need to accept that."

"But if you love him, then why can't you just get married? He's your boyfriend, isn't he?"

Honesty. The best policy, maybe. But seldom as easy

as it ought to be. "He *was* my boyfriend. But we've… broken up."

"But *why?*"

She opened her mouth to try to explain—and then shut it. There was no explaining why she loved Tucker but couldn't marry him, not to a ten-year-old boy. She said, "It didn't work out. That's all you need to know."

"Well, maybe you'll get back together again. If only you would—"

"Brody."

He knew that tone of voice and he'd learned that when she used it, she meant business. "What?" The tone was slightly sulky—but also, blessedly, less whiny than before.

"Marriage is not something the kids get to decide about. Do you understand?"

He bit his lip and looked down at the table. "Yeah."

"Tucker and I will still love you and take care of you, whether we're married or not."

"But Dad said—"

"Stop." With a sinking feeling low in her stomach, Lori realized she was going to have to have a long talk with Tucker before she left. She had to make him understand that granting Brody's every slightest wish had to stop. Already Lori could see the changes in her son: the whining when he didn't get his way, the demands that the adults in his life arrange their priorities to suit his own ten-year-old idea of how things ought to be.

It wasn't good.

And she knew that when she left, it would only get worse. Without her around to provide a little balance,

Brody was only going to become more and more certain that he ran the world. After all, he'd have Tucker to constantly remind him that he merely had to hint at wanting something and it would instantly be his.

"I'm sorry that you're disappointed," she said. "I truly am. But, Brody, sometimes things just don't work out the way you want them to."

After Brody was in bed that night, she tracked Tucker down in his study, where he sat at his big desk, busy at his computer. He didn't look up from the screen when she stepped over the threshold and shut the door behind her.

"Tucker." Finally, he granted her a glance. A distinctly icy one. "I need to talk to you."

He grunted and kept clicking the mouse, his eyes on the screen. "Seems to me like it's all pretty much been said."

"This isn't about you and me. It's about Brody."

"Brody…" *Click, click, click.* "*Now* you consider him…."

Anger like acid burned in her belly, made little prickly sensations along her limbs. She ordered it away. She had a goal here and losing her temper wouldn't help her achieve it. "That was cruel," she said levelly, and waited. He sent her another hard glance. She lifted her chin and waited some more. At last, after more clicking, he let go of the damn mouse and leaned back in his big leather chair. Now she had his attention, she said, "I do consider Brody. Always. With every breath I take."

"He's upset." It was an accusation.

She swallowed a sharp retort and schooled her voice to a reasonable tone. "Just think about that a little, will you? Think about *why* he's upset right now."

"Because you won't do the right thing, that's why."

"No. He's upset because you promised him something that you can't deliver. You promised him something you had no right to promise him." She could hear the heat building in her voice. She fell silent, breathed evenly, thought of cool running water, of the wind in the trees on a breezy summer day, of things that were soothing and calm. And as she tried to gather serenity around her, he just sat there, in his chair. Watching her.

Judging her? Actually listening now? She didn't know. His expression was impossible to read.

She tried again. "Oh, Tucker. I know you're angry with me, way deep down and maybe forever, for not doing everything I could to find you for all those years. And you're even angrier because I said no when you wanted to get married." She paused. Waiting for what? She wasn't sure. He still said nothing, so she went on, "I can't go back and do the past over. And I won't marry you when you can't forgive me. So that leaves us living separate lives and yet still needing to find some way to raise our son into a person who can be a…a happy and productive adult." She paused again. And again, he said nothing. She lifted both hands and let them drop, feeling about as hopeless as a person can feel. "Oh, Tucker. I tried to explain this to you before, about how you can't just hand him every little thing his heart desires and not have him start expecting that he'll always get everything he wants."

More awful silence. He looked her up and down—a long, slow pass from the top of her head to her sandaled feet and back up again. Even with it all so wrong between them, she felt the shimmer of heat, spreading out from her midsection, making her body burn.

Then, at last, he spoke. "All right. Yeah. Maybe you've got a point."

Shock that he'd come so close to agreeing with her made her knees go wobbly. There was a sofa against the wall not far from the door. She ordered her shaking legs to take her over there and lowered herself carefully onto it. Once seated, she dared to suggest, "It's not only about all the stuff you buy him…"

He shocked her again—by knowing exactly what she meant. "You and me." He shook his head. "I guess I kind of blew it, didn't I, talking to him about it before I talked to you?"

She nodded. "It gave him the idea that our getting married—or not—is up to him."

Tucker shifted in his chair. "Yeah," he said. "All right. Point taken." He frowned. She held her breath. And then he said, "Tell you what. I'll think twice in the future—about what he does or doesn't have a say in. And I'll stop burying him in electronic devices."

She couldn't help smiling—a quivery smile. But quivery or not, that smile felt good. Really good. In a bittersweet kind of way. "Sounds like a plan."

"Another thing…"

"Sure."

"Could you stay until soccer camp is over? He and I can handle Disneyland just between the two of us, I think."

Disneyland. She'd forgotten. And she'd been looking forward to it, too: to the three of them, on a family vacation…

But no. They weren't *that* kind of family. It wouldn't be good for any of them to pretend that they were.

He added, "And I need to start thinking about hiring someone to keep an eye on him during the day…"

So many changes.

None of them easy.

And what about her own life? It would be vastly different with Brody living here in the Junction so much of the time. Vastly different in a scary, empty sort of way. She'd need to make some changes, start really looking into getting herself something worthwhile to do with her days…

But not right this minute. Uh-uh. Right now, she needed to keep focused on this fragile new understanding between her and Tucker. They were building something here; they were taking their first baby steps as parents who would not also be husband and wife.

She suggested, "He's got friends on my mother's street—Peter and the other boys. My mom might be willing to let him stay with her while you're working. At least she might some days, anyway."

He almost smiled. "That's a great idea."

"I'll talk to her tomorrow, if you'd like me to."

"I would. And will you stay, then, here at the ranch, until soccer camp is over?"

"I'd be glad to."

* * *

Lori talked to her mother the next day. It went pretty well. Enid put on a little pressure, to get her to stay in town, to try to work things out with Tucker.

But Lori held firm. She was leaving. And would her mother like to watch Brody during the day while he was staying with his father?

"Oh, honey. Any time. You know that."

So it was arranged.

After she got things worked out with Enid, Lori went to see her sister. Lena was not pleased.

"Oh, that is crazy. That is just insane and disgusting and wrong. Honey, you love that man. You said so yourself two days ago…"

Lori tried to explain. "He doesn't trust me, not in his heart. And he's still angry with me. I have totally and completely blown it with him and he'll never forgive me."

"Oh, poo. Of course he'll forgive you—eventually. Yeah, you did a real bad thing. You know it. He knows it. So now you're both going to throw away your chance at a really *good* thing? Where's the sense in that? I've got a mind to go have a little talk with Tucker Bravo."

"Lena. Please don't."

"But honey. You *love* him."

"That's right. I do. And I'm not going to marry him. It wouldn't be good for me—or for Tucker, or for Brody—if I were to marry someone who resents me in his heart. Believe me, if I could make Tucker forgive me, I would. But you know I can't. That's up to him."

"Well, isn't he the biggest fool in Texas? And I don't see why you won't just let me—"

"Lena. No."

Lena argued some more. But in the end she promised to spare Tucker the sharp side of her tongue.

The final week went by. Lori had several long talks with Brody. He seemed to be over his whining and sulking and moving on to acceptance that his mother was not going to marry his newfound dad.

Lori and Tucker were gentle with each other—even friendly, in a cautious kind of way. By tacit agreement they steered clear of each other when Brody wasn't around.

And though she was still staying in his house and saw him every day, Lori missed him. So much. She missed his laughter and his kisses, his warm body close to hers in the dark hours of the night...

By that final Saturday morning, as she packed her things to leave, she found she was almost grateful to be getting out; to be headed home where there would be no reminders of him. *Home,* she thought, and pictured her spacious Spanish-style house—and realized that it didn't feel like home to her at all. Not anymore. Somehow, during her summer in the Junction, she'd slipped into thinking that home was right here again—where she'd grown up; where Tucker was.

Henry came to mind. She remembered him—his goodness, his gentleness, his caring ways—with a soft, sad little smile. It had been bad, getting over losing him. And now she would have to find a way to get over Tucker.

Neatly, she folded up the rest of her clothes. Jesse, who took care of the Double T garage and the fleet of

Cadillacs the Bravo brothers owned, came upstairs and took her suitcases down and put them in the Lexus.

Brody and Tucker came out to say goodbye. Lori hugged her son and told him she'd see him in a few weeks. She aimed a brave smile at Tucker, who stood a few feet away. "You guys have fun in Disneyland."

"We will. Love you, Mom." For a sweet, too-brief moment, Brody's young arms held her tight. Then he stepped back to stand by his father.

They lingered in the driveway, side-by-side—the love her secret had lost her, and her only child—as she drove off. She looked once in the rearview mirror and saw them standing there. Her throat clutched and her lungs ached as if somehow she'd sucked in ground glass.

After that one glance, she kept her eyes strictly front until she reached the bend in the driveway that obscured them from her view.

Chapter Eighteen

By the time Tucker and Brody got back from Disneyland a week and a day after Lori left for San Antonio, Tate's Junction was abuzz.

The story had leaked out at last—that Tucker Bravo was the father of Lori Billingsworth Taylor's love child. At Molly's salon, Prime Cut, all the ladies were talking.

Emmie Lusk was aghast. "So *that's* why she took that child and moved in at the ranch…"

Betty Stoops clucked her tongue and announced in obvious disapproval, "All those years and we never even knew it."

Emmie shook her head. "And now, I hear she's left town again. Just picked up and went back to San Antonio and left that little boy behind with Tucker." Emmie paused to simper and sigh. "That Tucker is one handsome hunk of manliness, I will admit." She scowled. "But what does he know about taking care of an impressionable child?"

"Well," Betty reminded them all, in the interest of fairness. "The boy *is* his son…"

There were murmurs of reluctant agreement all around.

Donetta Brewer, sitting in Molly's styling chair, gave Tate's wife a long look in the mirror. But Molly, who knew how to keep her mouth shut when nothing she said would make any difference anyway, only smiled pleasantly and snipped away at Donetta's hair.

"She'll be back," Donetta decreed. "She'll be back, just wait and see."

Tucker wanted Lori back.

He wanted her with him, at his side, day to day. He wanted his ring on her finger. He wanted her last name to be *his* name.

He wanted her there in his bed, every night, all womanly softness and tender caresses and sweet, sexy sighs. He wanted the taste of her mouth and the tiny, pleading cries she made when he loved her. He wanted to look across the dinner table and find her blue eyes waiting, the corners of her sweet mouth lifting in a come-and-get-it smile.

And damn, did he ever want her steady hand with Brody. With Lori gone, it became instantly obvious that, when it came to Brody, someone had be the tough one, the one who said "no," now and then. That job now fell to Tucker. He made it a point to say no almost as often as he told his son yes.

Brody did seem to take it well. In a way, Brody seemed happier and more relaxed, now he understood that his dad was the boss.

Still. It had been a hell of a lot more fun showering him with presents, promising him the moon, and watching his eyes light up every time Tucker came home from work with a new and outrageously expensive toy.

Oh, yeah. Tucker missed Lori in a hundred ways.

But to get her to come back to him, he had to forgive her. And he just couldn't quite see his way clear to do that.

Once or twice he'd considered calling her, faking it, telling her he loved her and he was over what she'd done.

But it would have been a whopping lie and she would have caught him out in it eventually. He wasn't over all the years she'd kept his son from him. He didn't think he'd ever be. Every time he looked at Brody, the awareness of the truth she'd hid from him caused a hollow spot beneath his ribs, an emptiness carved out by the years he had lost, the years he hadn't been there for Brody. Because of her.

Okay, yeah. Maybe he did love her. Maybe he had no choice in that. He couldn't stop himself from loving her. But there was a deep anger in the way he loved her, a bitter edge to his longing for her.

Twice, Brody had called her from their hotel room in Anaheim. Tucker listened to his son chatter away, giving her blow-by-blow descriptions of all the rides and attractions—and he'd wanted to snatch the phone from Brody's hands, to talk to her, tell her…

What?

He had to get past this. There was nothing to say.

The minute they'd come in from the car on Sunday, Brody had called her again. Tucker forced himself to leave the room. There was no point in standing there, listening to Brody's end of the conversation, furious and full of frustrated longing. It was better, he realized, just *not* to be there while Brody talked to her.

The week crawled by. Enid took care of Brody Monday through Friday. She was kind to Tucker, inviting him in, offering him coffee or a cold drink. He always politely refused. To be in her house—the house where Lori had grown up—brought back old memories, vague remembrances of Lori as a teenager, when he'd hardly known she existed. She used to wear her hair pulled back, didn't she? And she would smile at him, a hopeful, shy smile, when he came to see Lena.

Looking back over those long-ago times, he felt so lonely, had such a grim sense of missed connections. She'd said she'd loved him, even then—or at least, she'd had a heavy-duty crush on him. What might have happened if he'd had the sense, then, to look twice?

No. No point in what-ifs. And no way was he hanging out at Enid's house. He'd drop Brody off at eight-thirty and pick him up at five and head straight for the ranch.

Nights were the worst. With the workday over and Brody safely tucked into bed, Tucker was left alone, missing Lori, wanting to call her and demand that she come back to him, knowing such a stupid move would get him nowhere, fast.

Friday night he joined his brother in Tate's office for

a whiskey and a little conversation. Big mistake. They'd barely poured their drinks and put their feet up when Tate started in on him, demanding to know what the hell was going on with Lori.

"I thought you were planning to marry that woman. Hell, Tuck. What went wrong?"

Tucker was just miserable enough by then to tell his brother everything—how he couldn't forgive her for what she'd done, how he'd proposed anyway, but she'd turned him down. How she had some ridiculous idea that she couldn't live with him and be happy until he could let go of his resentment toward her.

Once the sad story was told, Tucker sat back, sipped his whiskey and waited for Tate to express a little brotherly sympathy. He waited for nothing.

"What's the deal?" Tate growled. "All of a sudden, you ain't got the sense to spit downward? You better look back, little brother. Look back on your sorry self when you left this town. You couldn't wait to shake the dust off your boots and get outta here. You *say* you would've stayed for Lori's sake, if she'd only been straight with you? Well, all right. Maybe you would've. And in a month—maybe two—you would've been miserable. You were bound and determined to blow this town and get a good look at the world outside of Texas. Time would have come—and it wouldn't have been long—when you would have been mad at that sweet woman for keepin' you here."

Tucker tried to make his hardheaded brother see the light. "It's not so much that she didn't tell me at first, before she knew about Brody. It's later. That's what gets me. When she had my baby and she didn't make the effort to—"

Tate didn't let him finish. "Okay. Say she'd tried harder to find you after Brody was born. What then?"

Tucker sat up straighter. "I would have come home."

"Yeah? So? I'm not saying you wouldn't have. You would have done right. I know that. You would have come home, married her, and settled down to play family man— when the last thing you were ready for back then was piles of dirty diapers and a young wife. How long d'you think that kind of marriage would have lasted?"

"I would have—"

Tate cut him off again. "Uh-uh, little brother. Things work out the way they work out. And if you look to the past with an honest eye, you're gonna see that you would have been just as mad at her back then for saddling you with a family that you weren't the least bit ready for, as you are now because she didn't tell you that you have a son."

"Damn it, I—"

"I'm not done yet. What's the matter with you? That was then and this is now and now is what you should be worrying about." Tate glowered and shook his head. "I thought you were smarter than this. I thought you knew that a man should never say no to the right woman's love. You want my advice?"

Tucker set down his half-full drink, lowered his boots to the floor and stood. "As a matter of fact, no."

"Too bad. You're gettin' it."

"Goodnight, Tate."

"I say get your butt to San Antonio." Tate shouted after him as Tucker headed out the door. "Tell that woman you love her and beg her to come back to you!"

So much for talking with Tate. Tucker wouldn't make that mistake again any time soon.

But the things Tate had said did kind of stick with him. They gnawed at him, all through that night and the sunny morning after. They made him remember a little more clearly the way he'd been back when, had him recalling that getting out of Tate's Junction *had* been important to him once. Even after he fell head-over-heels for Lori disguised as Lena, even while he was telling himself that he would stay there in town with her, after all…

Even then, the urge to get up and get out remained, pulling at him, laying within him the groundwork for regret if he had stayed. As it turned out, he'd left town anyway, with his heart broken.

But was Tate right? Was there more to it than he was seeing?

Was it just possible that, deeper even than heartbreak, there'd also been a certain anticipation? Yeah, he'd lost the woman he wanted. But he was also getting free of his mean old granddaddy; walking away from the town that called him the bastard Bravo boy behind his back.

Saturday after lunch, Tucker went to his study. He played Spider Solitaire and continued to ponder what his brother had said.

He'd been staring at his computer screen for maybe twenty minutes, when Brody appeared in the doorway to the front hall. He held up his bike helmet. "I'm gettin' out for a while, Dad. Gonna ride my bike."

Tucker nodded, hardly glancing over. "Have fun."

"You bet."

Brody left. Tucker pulled up another game and went after it, all the while brooding on the painful points Tate had made. He couldn't have said how long he sat there, recalling the past and his own part in it, finishing one game and bringing up the next. Maybe a half hour, maybe more.

When the phone rang, he almost left it for Mrs. Haldana. And then he remembered that she'd taken the weekend off to visit her son and his family in Abilene. On the third ring he grabbed it.

"Hello. This is Tucker."

"Omigod." A woman's voice, one he didn't recognize. A breathless, scared-sounding voice. "Oh, Mr. Bravo…"

"Who is this?"

"Aileen Martino."

"Sorry. The name doesn't ring a bell…"

"I live in town. But that doesn't matter. I…Mr. Bravo. I'm out on the state road, at the foot of your driveway. Your son's here with me. I've called an ambulance."

The bottom fell out of the world. All he could do was stupidly repeat, "An ambulance…"

"Yes. Oh, I'm so sorry. Mr. Bravo, there's been an accident…"

Chapter Nineteen

Lori had just let herself in the house with her arms full of groceries, when she got Tucker's call. She listened to what he had to tell her and asked a few pertinent questions. Once she had the answers she needed, she promised to be there as soon as she could.

She hung up—and then she just stood there, leaning on the kitchen counter, trying to catch her breath.

As soon as she felt she could walk without falling over, she considered the groceries. She should put them away. She began emptying the bags—and then, with a box of Wheat Thins in one hand and a loaf of bread in the other—she froze.

Who cared about the groceries at time like this?

She dropped the box and the loaf on the counter,

grabbed her purse and her keys, went back out through the kitchen door to the garage and got in behind the wheel of the Lexus.

She made it to the Junction in record time. Yes, she broke a few speed limits—more than a few, actually. But she arrived at Tate Memorial in one piece and without a single speeding ticket. It was a little after eight in the evening when she entered Brody's room.

"Mom! You're here!" Her son was sitting up in bed, a cast on one arm and a cut on his swollen lip. Beneath the blankets, she could see the lumpy shape of a leg cast. He held out his good arm to her.

She ran to him and he let her hug him. She did it gently, sucking in the dusty boy-smell of him, reveling in the feel of his arm squeezing her neck—and biting back grateful tears.

A broken arm and a broken leg. Various cuts and bruises...

But he would be okay. She'd known it when she talked to Tucker. Still, it had been necessary to see for herself, to get here as fast as she could and hold him in her aching arms.

He would be all right...

And he was squirming in her hold. "Okay, Mom. Don't *strangle* me."

Knowing she couldn't hold on forever, she let him go. "Oh." She whipped a tissue out of the box on the bed tray and blew her nose, dabbed at her eyes. "Just look at you..."

"Aw, Mom..."

She noticed Tucker then, as he swept to his feet from the chair in the corner.

Tucker. Just the sight of him broke her heart anew. He looked like a man who'd seen death coming at him with grasping, greedy arms. She glanced at their battered little boy and supposed it was no surprise that his father was a wreck.

"I'll be in the waiting room." He was at the door in two long strides—and gone before she could think of what to say to him.

And by then, Brody was chattering away between sips of the orange juice one of the nurses must have brought him. He showed her the straw. "Sweet, huh? With a bend in the middle? I like a flex straw. I really do." She pulled the chair over beside him and dropped into it and listened to him tell her how he hadn't *really* gone beyond the driveway. Not on purpose, anyway. "But I got to the end of it and I was going a little bit too fast and I couldn't stop in time and this lady in this great, big SUV came down the road and—bam—she got me." He groaned. "Oh, Mom. Did it hurt. And that poor lady, Mrs. Martino, I felt real sorry for her. She was scared that she'd killed me or something. But I told her, 'I'm okay. But my arm doesn't work and my leg really hurts and I think you better get me to the hospital now.' So I made her get out her cell phone. She was, you know, really freaking. I made her dial nine-one-one. And then, after that, I gave her Dad's number and told her to her call him."

"Good thinking," Lori said, beaming through a fresh flood of tears.

Brody played with his straw and took a sip and then set it down on the tray. "Mom. I'm sorry. I know I was going too fast. I know I wasn't careful."

She gave him her most serious expression and she nodded, slowly. "That's right. You weren't."

"I'll never do something like that again. I promise."

"Good," she said, though she was thinking that it was probably the kind of promise a ten-year-old boy would have a hard time keeping. There would be more cuts and scrapes and bruises. That was part of being a kid. She only prayed that there would never again be anything so scary she had to break every speed limit in Texas getting to his side.

Brody leaned back against the fat white pillow. His eyes were drooping. She realized that they would have given him something for the pain, something that seemed to be catching up with him now. "I'm not gonna play soccer this year, am I?"

"There's always next year."

He almost smiled. "I knew you'd say that—and I feel kinda tired, you know?"

She nodded, put her hand on his forehead, felt the warmth and the velvety smoothness of his skin. "Rest, then."

"Mom…" He crooked a finger—on the hand that wasn't half-covered by a cast. She leaned in closer. He whispered, "You'd better go deal with Dad, I think. He's pretty crazed about this whole thing."

Tucker jumped from the waiting room chair at the sight of her. And then he just stood there, hanging his golden head, the picture of misery and raging guilt.

He started accusing himself. "Lori. What can I tell you? It's all my fault, I know that. I know you blame me. And you're right—right to blame me. I hardly even looked up when he said he was going out to ride that bike. I just waved him away and—"

"Stop."

He hung his head even lower, big shoulders slumping. "Yeah. Okay. I know. You don't want to hear it. And I don't see why you should."

A sweet-looking white-haired lady sat nearby, knitting—or at least, she *had* been knitting, before she got interested in watching Tucker beat himself up.

Lori stepped a little closer to him. Gently, she took his hand. He stiffened—and then he grabbed on tight. "Let's go outside," she said.

He looked at her then. She saw the dawning of hope in his beautiful eyes. "Yeah. Okay. Outside..."

They found a bench in the shadows on the side of the building, around from the main entrance, next to a big planter full of bright pink and purple impatiens.

The second they were seated, Tucker started in on himself again. "I should have been paying more attention. He went out and I—"

"Tucker."

He let out a hard breath. "What?"

"You did nothing wrong. And there's no reason to blame yourself. He's ten years old. You can't watch him every moment. He knew to stay away from the road. He just admitted to me that he wasn't careful. And he wasn't."

"But I—"

She dared to reach out, to press her fingers to his lips.

She broke the tender contact almost instantly, but still, she felt the fire, the little surge of magical heat that passed between them whenever they touched. "Listen. Are you listening?" He gulped and nodded. "It's not your fault. Accidents happen sometimes. And we can thank the good Lord that all Brody's got from this one is a couple of broken bones. We can tell him to be more careful. And after this, I'll bet he will be. But don't even think that I blame you, because I don't."

Tucker stared at her—well, gaped, was more the word for it. "You mean that? You're not blaming me?"

"Of course not." She scooted closer, close enough to nudge his shoulder with her own. "He's going to be okay." She faked a gruff voice. "So lighten up."

He shut his eyes, whispered, "Lori…"

Something in his tone made her heartbeat quicken. "Yeah?" She hardly dared to breathe.

He leaned back on the bench, tipped his head up, and looked at the darkening sky above. "I never knew my father. But still, I hated him. I swore I'd never be like him—making kids all over the damn place. And then just walking away. That's why I've been so furious at you, I think. Not because you never managed to track me down and tell me that I had a son. But because the way it turned out, I'm just like my own dad. I got you pregnant. And then I was gone."

"You didn't walk away from Brody, Tucker. You had no choice. I gave you none."

He took his gaze off the sky then, and looked at her squarely. "It all worked out, though, didn't it?"

"Oh, I'd like to think that it did."

"Yeah. It did work out. I got away from the Junction. And then I got to *choose* to come home. And you gave my son a good father while I was gone—a man who really loved you the way you deserve to be loved. A man who took care of you, of both of you, better than I could have at the time. And now, here you are, beside me, and all I can think of is that all that—what you did, what I *didn't* do. None of that matters. All I can think is that we should be together, now. That you're the only woman for me and you always have been. And that, as far as forgiveness goes, well, if you need to hear me say it, I do forgive you. But right now, I can't see that there's anything to forgive." He took her hand once more. "Lori. I love you."

She felt the tears welling again, and gently swiped them away. "Oh. I'm so glad."

"Do you remember that first night you and Brody came out to the ranch?"

"Yes. Yes, of course I do."

"That night, I tried to tell you something—something so important."

"But I wouldn't let you. I couldn't. Not then."

"Can you let me tell you now?"

She had to swipe more tears away. "Yes. Oh, yes. I can."

"Lori. That first day you came back to town, when I saw you getting out of that fine silver car, I thought, *There. Right there. At last. Now I know the reason I came back to my hometown.*" He hooked an arm around her and pulled her close. "You're the reason, Lori. It's you. Always. You."

"Oh, Tucker. I do love you so."

"Marry me. Move back here, to the Junction—or if you don't want that, we can—"

She touched his mouth again. "Shh. I'd love to move back home and live at the ranch with you and Brody. That works for me. And my sister will plan our wedding. How else could it be? And I'm thinking that I want to go back to school, get a business degree. But these days, you can do that online, so that should be no problem at all." She beamed up at him. "Kiss me. Do it now."

He chuckled. "You haven't said yes yet."

"Oh, Tucker. I've been saying yes for weeks now. And finally. At last. You are hearing me." She twined her arms around his neck and lifted her mouth.

And he kissed her. A kiss of passion and commitment. Of love and forgiveness. A kiss rich with the promise of all the days to come—*their* days, together. At last.

* * * * *

SPECIAL EDITION™

Coming in June 2005
the second book in reader favorite

Christine Flynn's

compelling new miniseries

**This quiet Vermont town inspires old lovers
to reunite—and new loves to blossom!**

THE SUGAR HOUSE
SE #1690, available June 2005

Jack Travers returns to his childhood home to find his
old neighbor Emmy Larkin and make up for his father's
scandalous betrayal of her father years ago. Emmy had
always been like a baby sister to Jack. Now she's all
grown up, and the sight of her turns his protective
instincts into something more primal....

Don't miss this emotional story—only from Silhouette Books!

Where love comes alive™

This June

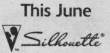

SPECIAL EDITION™

Presents the exciting finale
of the continuity

MONTANA MAVERICKS

GOLD RUSH GROOMS

Lucky in love—and striking it rich—
beneath the big skies of Montana!

MILLION-DOLLAR MAKEOVER
by Cheryl St.John

In the ultimate rags-to-riches story, plain-Jane Lisa Martin
learns that she's inherited the Queen of Hearts gold mine.
Yet the idea of being rich and powerful is foreign to the
quiet, bookish young woman. So when handsome
Riley Douglas offers to join her payroll and manage the
property, Lisa is grateful. But is Riley too good to be true?

Available in June 2005 at your favorite retail outlet.

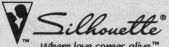

Where love comes alive™

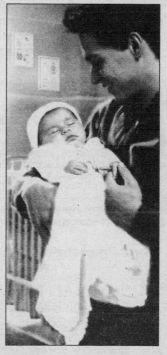

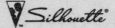